Praise for 'The Popping

This is the kind of book  story line grabs you and .... you loose. It certainly does not disappoint. I fish those islands and was delighted to see the detail of description when introducing the reader to the beauty of this part of Florida.......

Captain Terry Vander Meer

Mr. Grant has created not only a "keep you guessing" murder mystery, with plenty of colorful characters, but he has also given his reader an insight into life in Southwest Florida. The setting is perfect for this kind of story, complete with great descriptions of the laid-back lifestyle in a little town where nothing ever happens; well, almost never. A great book for the beach, or poolside, of in front of a warm fireplace. I can't wait for Mr. Grant's next offering.

Carl D. Megill

Terrific read! Couldn't put the book down! This book has romance, suspense, and history rolled into one. Definitely recommend reading!!!!

Carol Faircloth

Praise for 'The Cut Bait Murders'

If you enjoy a suspense story mixed together with a dash of history, a cup or two of humor that is shaken- not stirred- on an island off the southwestern coast of Florida, you will love Mitch Grant's latest addition to his Pine Island Mysteries. 'The Cut Bait Murders' is a page turning adventure filled with characters that pull you along as they try to solve the disappearance of fellow islanders.

Pati B. Vander Meer

Great read! Mitch Grant puts you in St. James City, and the rest of Pine Island. You could easily taste the island's food and drinks, and you become one with the residents... Mr. Grant also sticks in some history of the island, but doesn't bore you. You want to be there. I loved it. Hurry up and write another book.

"JuJu"

The SILVER SPOON MURDER

A St James City Mystery

MITCH GRANT

ISBN: 1508499578
ISBN 13: 9781508499572
Library of Congress Control Number: 2015903145
CreateSpace Independent Publishing Platform
North Charleston, South Carolina

The book is a work of fiction. It does, however, make reference to real places of business on the islands of Southwest Florida's Gulf Coast. I have attempted to describe them as faithfully as possible, recognizing, however, that I could never do justice to just how pleasant and delightful they actually are. I apologize in advance for shortcomings in this regard, and urge you to visit these establishments and determine this for yourself.

The book also makes reference to Florida's sugar industry. While the names of companies used in this work are fictitious I have attempted to describe the agricultural practices of this industry as accurately as possible, relying on many different publicly available sources of information to guide my descriptions. The names of individuals depicted as owning and/or managing these enterprises are purely fictitious, and the opinions and actions I have depicted them taking are fictitious and are solely my inventions.

In all other respects this novel is a work of fiction. Names, characters, places, and incidents are either the product of the author's imagination or are used fictitiously. Any resemblance to actual persons, living or dead, or to actual events, locales, or organizations is unintentional and coincidental.

Finally, I want to express my appreciation to my friends and neighbors on the island who, despite the real risk of some aspects of their characters being incorporated into one of my books, continue to be willing to occasionally associate with my wife and me.

This book is dedicated to the memory of **Marjory Stoneman Douglas**, the author who, long before most, saw the need to educate Floridians, and the World, about the State's treasure known as the Everglades. I urge all to seek out a copy of her masterwork- **'The Everglades: River of Grass.'**

"If Okeechobee and the lakes and marshes north that contribute to it, if rivers and swamps and ponds had not existed to hoard all that excess water in a great series of reservoirs by which the flow was constantly checked and regulated, there would have been no Everglades. The whole system was like a set of scales on which the forces of the seasons, of the sun and the rains, the winds, the hurricanes, and the dewfalls, were balanced so that the life of the vast grass and all it encompassed and neighbor forces were kept secure."

- The Everglades: River of Grass. America's Unique Natural Treasure, by Marjory Stoneman Douglass

Cover Art

The Eve of Destruction- an original painting by Mel Meo.

Mel Meo is an artist whose work embodies the peace of Pine Island, Florida, her home for forty years. The painter learned to draw as a child sitting on top of abandoned Calusa Indian mounds that surrounded her family's home. Her paintings today, still reflecting the influence and spirit of that setting, are eclectic and exuberant, bursting forth through an astounding variety of mediums and surfaces, and always exhibiting the artist's spirituality and sense of humor. Mel often paints from dreams or themes that seem to spring from some inner journey pushing her, always, toward the mysterious good or another beginning. Mel describes the experience as like opening the door.

Her studio's address is:
    Mel Meo Studio
    Pine island Center
    melmeostudio@yahoo.com
    239-283-0236

Chapter One

Some days on the water are better than others.

We were boating up the sound. On board were Kenny, his wife, Janice, Janice's sister, Gigi, my wife, Jill, and me. The morning had started well enough. The sun was shining, the wind nothing more than a breeze, and the surface of the sound glassy. In other words, it was a perfect day for boating.

We were on our way to Doc Ford's restaurant on Captiva Island. We like to go there–the food's great and the drink selection will satisfy whatever you're thirsting for. The ladies, as was their nature, had seen the outing as a good reason to dress in some of their nicer boating attire. Jill had selected a favorite androsia-print sleeveless blouse along with white shorts. Janice and Gigi both had their own versions of attractive tropical print outfits atop either spotless white shorts or stylish Capri pants.

Those who don't live full-time in a quiet fishing village on the southern tip of a remote, undeveloped Southwest Florida island probably can't appreciate just how big a deal it is to have an opportunity to go 'off-island.' The ladies were looking forward to a fun day.

And those who don't live near the coast probably don't pay much attention to tides. But if you're a boater, you have to, and that's especially true for those who venture onto Pine Island Sound. To the novice this body of water looks like a huge aquatic play ground: roughly twenty miles long and three miles wide. But when the dimension of water depth is considered, the skipper's options become more limited. Today that was especially true because the tide was in a negative state by about half a foot. It was a bad low!

Generally, I like to boat in these conditions since the low tide allows you to see where the shallow areas really are. When it's like this, many of the bars actually stick out of the water, and the others are usually visible just below the surface.

Whenever I have enough water I always try to avoid the channel so that I don't have to deal with the chop and waves stirred up by the wakes of those captains who want to, or have to, stay in it. But today, due to the negative tide, I didn't really have a choice. I was staying as far to the right side of the channel as I could, not only because that is the correct way to navigate, but also so that I would minimize the impact of my boat's wake on the tarpon fishermen who were anchored on the left edge of the channel. But, as I looked ahead, I suspected that the impact of his boat's wake was the furthest thing from the mind of the skipper whose boat was heading in our direction—a boat at least seventy feet long and traveling at more than thirty knots. All it took was a glance to tell that the wake spewing from the boat's stern was serious. Even from a distance I could see this was not a wave to be trifled with. But I assumed that the guy would slow down before he came down the narrow gap between the boats fishing on the left and my bay boat skirting the sand bar on the right.

That assumption would prove to be wrong! And, in retrospect, it was clearly a mistake. Now I had to deal with the consequences of that mistake. The wake heading our way was at least six feet high, and moving at more than thirty knots. My choices were limited. I couldn't go to the right—the water there was too thin. I didn't have time to spin and run. The only thing I could do was slow down and ease the boat, at a slight angle, into the face of the wave. I yelled at the ladies sitting on the bow's cushions to hang on and silently watched as the wake approached. Perhaps, I thought to myself, I should have suggested they stand up and hang on. But, by then, it was too late.

The bow climbed the oncoming sea. Within seconds it pointed toward the sky. Then it pointed just as steeply downward. But, so far, no problem. The boat rode the first wake perfectly. Everyone was still dry, but the boat could not deal with the secondary sea in the same fashion. The bow stuck itself squarely into the face of the oncoming wake, a sizeable amount of which came on board. Now, not only was there a lot of green water in the boat, there was also a lot of green water on top of the nicely dressed ladies who had been so looking forward to their day off-island.

As I was dealing with the consequences of almost being swamped, I turned to look at the passing cruiser. As soon as I could take my hands off the boat's controls, I raised them to vigorously relay a couple of 'you're number one' salutes, but there was no sign that the skipper was paying attention. The only response was from one of the several bikini-clad females lounging on the craft's upper level sun deck. She timidly waved, shrugged her shoulders, and held up her beer can, as if she was trying to apologize by offering me one. I ground my teeth. The only other thing I noticed was the lettering on the boat's stern as, through a haze of diesel fumes and salt spray, it disappeared toward Ft. Myers. There, proudly displayed in bright gold script, sparkling in the morning sunlight, was the yacht's name, "Sugar."

Some days on the water are better than others.

Chapter Two

The ladies were troopers. They all bought into my suggestion that the warm sun and the wind flow from the boat traveling at speed would dry them off in no time. As soon as things settled down and the water drained out of the boat, I put it onto a plane and we again headed toward Captiva.

To help with the drying process, I ran faster than my normal cruising speed. I figured the girls would probably appreciate this thoughtfulness, but I didn't sense much appreciation, possibly due to the effect of the wind on their hair. Certainly, any appreciation for my boating skills disappeared entirely after what happened next.

I had made the run to Captiva's entrance channel many times and never had a problem. I usually ran a straight line from the east side of the power lines toward the cell tower that sticks up on that island's northern tip. Granted, there's some shallow stuff on the west side of the channel, but nothing that ever gave me trouble. Running north I noticed a couple of flats skiffs ahead, but because there was a bit of space between them, I figured I could split the distance and not cause either any problem. I certainly hadn't planned to provide them the best laughs they've probably ever had. What I didn't know, and what hadn't shown on my GPS chart, was that they were fishing on separate sides of an underwater mound that stuck up above the level of the surrounding bottom; a hump that stuck up just enough to graze the bottom of my engine as it moved us toward Captiva Island at a faster than normal clip.

The boat came to a stop before I had time to react. So there we were, stuck on a sand bar in the middle of the bay. In the span of no more than five minutes, I had managed not only to drench the ladies in salt water, but also strand us between two boats of laughing fishermen.

Jill was clearly not amused. I suspected that neither were any of my other passengers, although they were far too polite to let that show. At that point our only option was for Kenny and me to jump in and try to push the boat off the shoal. Fortunately, once we learned to push in the same direction at the same time, we were able to reach water deep enough to float the boat and run the outboard. Soon, we were again underway, but now, not only were the ladies soaked, but so were Kenny and me.

As I mentioned before, some days on the water are better than others.

Chapter Three

Jill and I retired a little over two years ago and moved to our newly purchased home in St. James City, Florida, a tiny fishing village located on the southern tip of Pine Island. When people ask where this island is located we tell them that it's between Sanibel and Ft. Myers. While that's not strictly correct from a geographic standpoint, it does give a general idea of where we live, and because of the reference to Sanibel Island, conveys a sense of tropical exclusivity and status. But that's not strictly correct either.

Pine Island has a couple of claims to fame. One is that it's the largest island in the state of Florida, stretching north to south about eighteen miles. At its widest point, it's maybe two miles across. It's also one of the state's least densely populated islands for a couple of reasons. First, there are no beaches on Pine Island. Second, what we do have plenty of are mosquitoes and mangroves, neither of which matches that romantic tropical image those looking to relocate to Florida usually have in mind.

St. James City has a permanent year-round population of a few thousand folks, but during the winter months, or during "Season" as it's called, that number swells to four times that number. It could be coincidental, but during those cooler months our mosquito population is greatly reduced. Be that as it may, our favorite time of the year is the summer. Not only do we once again have the island, and its roads and restaurants, to ourselves, but it's the best time of the year for fishing and boating.

Another little known fact about St. James City is that it was the first incorporated city in this part of the state. It was founded shortly after the first tarpon ever caught on a rod and reel was subdued less than a mile away in the mouth of what today, appropriately enough, is called Tarpon Bay. This event produced an avalanche of national publicity, and as a consequence, the town enjoyed a brief period of fame and prosperity. But the aforementioned mosquitoes, along with the transportation difficulties one faced to get here, quickly convinced the brave souls who came here to fish they could have more fun elsewhere. So, after only a dozen years, St. James City failed and reverted to being a quiet, isolated, unincorporated village, which to this day, it remains. That's why we moved here.

Jill and I both grew up in small towns, and that's what we were looking for when we retired. We had both traveled the world enough to understand we'd been there, done that, and didn't need to go back. We were looking for a quiet place where we could boat, fish, and entertain our grandkids. And, for the most part, that's what we've found. We've got a boat hanging on a lift in the canal outside our back door, the fishing's always great, and the kids love to visit.

Chapter Four

One of the great things about living in a small town is that you make so many friends. I know that this statement seems counterintuitive. One might think that the larger the place you live, the more friends you will likely have, but, at least by our experience, that's not true. During our careers, despite having lived in some of the nation's largest cities, most of our friends there were those with whom we worked.

Probably, it's just that once you're retired you have more time, and indeed have a greater need to seek out those with similar interests. In some ways, it's kind of like going back to your childhood, back when you were in school. Now we have the time to be friendly again.

In that regard, Jill became great friends with a group of ladies roughly her age, with similar backgrounds and interests. One of the things they love to do is get together on a weekly basis and play cards. At least that's what they claim to be doing every Tuesday night. In reality, what they do is enjoy the evening's "signature" cocktail, share a gourmet meal that one of the members of the group has prepared, and catch up on the town's gossip. Sometimes they do actually play canasta, but they always seem to have fun.

Because this group is chartered as 'girls only,' the spouses have to find a way to occupy themselves on Tuesday nights. From time to time we get together to play poker. Sometimes we go to the American Legion to take part in that organization's fund raising scam known as "Show Me the Money." Sometimes we are just happy to stay home and enjoy the solitude, but one of the things I most look forward to is attending, on the first Tuesday of each month, the meetings of the Pine Island Improvement Association.

This group is, by far, the most influential civic group on the island. Its formal mission is to preserve the unique culture and character of life on Pine Island. In other words, it tries to make sure that politicians, developers, and other money-grubbers from the mainland don't come out here and screw it up for those of us lucky enough to already live here. It's a mission that I wholeheartedly support and tonight's meeting promised to be especially entertaining. I had been looking forward to it since I had heard who was to be the evening's speaker. Jay Benjamin, one of the region's most influential, outspoken, and engaging environmental activists, never failed to have something intelligent and controversial to say. I was looking forward to hearing his talk and to watching the members' reactions to his comments.

I arrived at the Elks Club fifteen minutes early, understanding the hall was likely to be packed. Even so, when I walked in, the place was already crowded. Fortunately, I was able to find an empty chair in the back of the room. What this spot lacked in terms of proximity to the speaker, it made up for in terms of the view of the crowd it gave me. My experience at previous meetings had shown it often could be entertaining to watch members respond to, and argue about, the speakers' messages. To be fair, if the topic was environmental, usually they didn't argue as much as they berated the speakers for not staking out even more extreme positions. I figured tonight would be more of the same, and I looked forward to an enjoyable and educational few hours.

Once I found a seat, I scanned the room to see who was there. It didn't take long to notice the group's president was in his usual spot near the head table. He's a competent and reasonable enough guy, even though he sometimes struggles to maintain decorum when the debates heat up. I noticed he was talking to the editor of the island's paper, another good guy, whom I figured was getting background information about the upcoming meeting. At a table in the corner I noticed a small crowd, not unusual because this was where guests were able to sample a free supply of homemade sweets and baked goods.

In that group I could make out several people I knew, including the owner of the island's only liquor store, a fellow with whom I was now on speaking terms, possibly due to having visited his establishment a little more frequently than was probably good for my liver. He seemed to be listening politely to Sandy Hampshaw, a fellow I knew to be one of the island's leading developers. Since arriving here, I had learned that, despite his profession, most on the island liked and respected him. Not only were his projects successful and profitable, but he also always appeared to go out of his way to ensure that they were environmentally responsible. A unique and likeable guy for sure.

I wasn't really surprised to see Sandy at the meeting. I had seen him interviewed on local television earlier in the day, answering questions about a new housing project he was putting together; a project that was going to need approval by the county's Planning Commission, a group that paid close attention to input from citizens' groups like the PIIA. It made sense he would be shaking as many hands and patting as many backs as he could. I had to smile.

I moved my gaze to the speaker's lectern where another small group had gathered. I immediately recognized one of the key members of the Association, a fellow by the name of Bill McClelland. Bill's a retired lawyer, dedicated conservationist, passionate environmentalist, and respected island expert. There was no question that Bill is a serious and important player on the island's environmental scene. I respected him for what he did for the island, and beyond that, for the way he seemed to approach these interests. Too often those of his persuasion come across as strident, shrill, and overly opinionated, doing little to disguise an obvious disbelief that anyone with an opinion contradictory to theirs could really be that stupid. But Bill wasn't like that. He always appeared to go out of his way to understand all sides of an issue and treat his opponents, and their opinions, with respect. I liked him for that. I also appreciated his reputation for tenacity and for not backing away from a fight over something about which he believed. For example, I knew that Bill was involved in litigation against the City of Cape Coral, having sued the city over its failure to address the large volume of polluted water flowing from city canals into the waters of Matlacha Pass.

Bill assisted Jay Benjamin in setting up a projector for the evening's presentation. As they worked, I saw they were chatting and laughing. It made sense that they knew and liked each other.

I also noticed a good-looking lady helping them set up by erecting the projection screen. I didn't know her name, but I recognized her from previous meetings. I knew her to be outspoken on any topic that she perceived to be a threat to the island, and she seemed especially fervent on the subject of dirty water from Cape Coral's canals. I remembered hearing that her house was located on Matlacha's Back Bay—a body of water particularly impacted by the outflow from the canals. I assumed that was the reason for what, in my opinion, were her frequently unrealistic and over-the-top positions on this subject. I had to admit that another reason I paid attention, though only as a disinterested observer, was the way she looked. She was probably in her late-fifties but, in my opinion, quite attractive. Her face was striking, even though it was beginning to display crow's feet around her eyes, probably earned from years of squinting into the bright Florida sun. A modest imperfection that only served to draw attention to her gorgeous hazel eyes—eyes that managed to convey both intelligence, and possibly, I thought, sadness.

I observed all three seemed to be on good terms: relaxed, smiling, and apparently enjoying each other's company, conveying a sense of being on the same team. When the set-up was complete she appeared to wish Jay Benjamin luck, patted him on the arm, and returned to her seat at a table near the front of the room. She sat next to a fellow that I assumed was her husband, a serious and professional looking gent. As I've gotten older I've found it more difficult to accurately judge the age of others, but I couldn't help but think he had to have been at least twenty years her senior. I noticed as she sat down she gave him the same pat on the arm.

By now the hall was standing room only. I gladly relinquished my seat to a late-arriving sprightly little dear who had to have been at least ninety, and assumed a position against the back wall—still a great spot from which to keep a close watch on the proceedings.

As the president gaveled the meeting to order, I noticed that Frank Osceola had arrived. He took a spot leaning against the wall to my left. We exchanged nods of recognition. I knew him casually from having attended parties hosted by mutual friends. At those gatherings I had learned a few important things about Frank. First, without question, he was one of the island's true characters. For starters, his nickname was 'Skunkfoot.' I knew that the boys at Froggy's, one of the island locals' favorite bars, had bestowed this moniker on him because of the awful smell of the white rubber fishing boots, better known down here as 'Matlacha Reeboks,' that he seemed to always wear. I had learned the guys at the bar always insisted that he leave his footwear outside before he came in to get a drink. I was very thankful to note tonight Frank was wearing flip flops and not his boots. Another unique thing about Frank was he was a full-blooded Seminole but, as he was quick to point out, he was not a member of the Seminole or Miccosukee 'tribes,' since he considered anyone who had signed the tribal documents to have surrendered to the U.S. government, and that was something he absolutely refused to do. Consequently, he wasn't entitled to receive the monthly stipend certified tribal members got from the proceeds of the group's gambling enterprises. You had to admire Frank for his principles. Besides, he didn't really need the money because he ran the island's barge service, an enterprise that ferried construction materials and other necessities of life out to bridgeless North Captiva. On his return trips he frequently brought back garbage. I loved it when he'd load a large propane tanker truck onto his barge and take it out to refill the island residents' gas tanks monthly. It was always a sight, when fishing on the flats, to look up and see what looked like a large truck driving across the water at a distance. I can't imagine how expensive it is to live on North Captiva, but it was a need that kept Frank profitably employed.

Another thing I knew about Frank was he had strong views about certain environmental issues, views that sometimes contradicted the more mainstream and politically acceptable views of most members of the Pine Island Improvement Association. I figured his presence at tonight's meeting might spice things up.

Chapter Five

The President spoke into the microphone, tested to make sure it was working, urged those standing near the cookie table to find their seats and, precisely at seven o'clock, gaveled the meeting to order. He asked for approval of the minutes of the previous meeting, which was unanimously granted, and asked the group's Treasurer to deliver a financial update. With those routines out of the way he recognized a number of special guests.

The first person he introduced was Mrs. Mildred Caldwell, asking the group to give her, a founding member of the organization, a round of applause for having recently celebrated her one hundredth birthday. Once the clapping stopped, she brought the house down by asking if someone would bring her another drink. The President then recognized a couple of men who had just come into the building and were standing near the entrance to the hall. The first person was introduced as the hardest working member of the Lee County Commission, the Honorable Lee Thunderburke. He was given a warm round of applause. The man standing to his side was introduced as the newest member of the Lee County Commission, the Honorable Kevin Powell. I knew that, in the most recent election, Powell had narrowly defeated tonight's speaker for a seat on the commission. The race had been noteworthy in that Powell's campaign had spent almost a million dollars on negative television advertisements that accused his opponent of everything from being a spendthrift to resembling a modern-day reincarnation of Carl Marx. Reportedly those ads had been funded by a PAC jointly supported by the sugar and phosphate industries, which was noteworthy because neither of these had a direct operating presence in Lee County. Consequently, despite Commissioner Powell's seemingly heartfelt assurances to the contrary, it was widely assumed that once in office he would not be especially friendly toward projects to protect the environment. This had proven to be true because, as soon as he had assumed office, his first vote had been to tap into a fund established to buy endangered wetlands and move the dollars into the general fund. All of this made his presence at tonight's meeting surprising, and the applause he received from the crowd was no more than polite.

With these pleasantries out of the way, the President recognized the program chairwoman to introduce the evening's speaker, which she did, although it might be more accurate to describe her introduction as more of a gushing of praise and admiration than the welcome traditionally given a speaker, but Jay Benjamin handled the compliments and enthusiastic applause that followed calmly and with no obvious sign of embarrassment. He waved to calm the crowd and quickly got down to business.

He opened his presentation with a question. "How many of you believe that acting to improve the quality of water in Southwest Florida's rivers and coastal estuaries is one of the most important priorities for our region?"

Not surprisingly, the show of hands that followed proved he was speaking to a largely receptive crowd. He, of course, indicated he was in agreement and went on to suggest that, in fact, our entire way of life on this coast was dependent upon clean waters, noting that not only was water important for drinking and the needs of daily living, but also critical to our fishing, swimming, boating, tourism, and real estate industries. By the time he finished his introductory remarks, I judged that everyone in the crowd bought into this thesis. Everyone, that is, but Commissioner Powell. I couldn't help but notice that his body language—slouching, tightly crossed arms, leaning away from the speaker—indicated that he probably wasn't totally on board with the speaker's comments. Commissioner Thunderburke, for his part, had a wry smile on his face and appeared to be enjoying his fellow public servant's discomfort. I thought that was a good sign, serving to reinforce my positive impression of the guy.

Benjamin continued with his presentation, using well-prepared, logical, and organized PowerPoint slides. He did an effective job of reviewing the history of water management in our region, describing in detail the historical events that had led to the creation of the region's water management structures. One slide showed how the waters in Florida historically had drained from around what is now Orlando, down the Kissimmee River, through Lake Okeechobee, into the Everglades, and on into Florida Bay, describing as he did Florida's famous "River of Grass," the ecological marvel described lovingly by Marjorie Stoneman Douglas in her magnificent book of the same name.

He went on to discuss the death and destruction south of the lake caused by the great hurricane of 1928, a category five storm that had pushed the lake's waters over its surrounding dikes, flooding hundreds of thousands of acres, and drowning more than three thousand souls; a disaster that led to the construction of the massive earthen berms that now surrounded the lake and to the dredging of outflows to direct excess water into the Gulf and the Atlantic. At the time, those engaged in this effort thought they were doing a great thing because, not only would this construction control floods, it would also allow safe water passage from one coast to the other, while stopping the flow of water south of the lake allowing the rich muck of the Everglades to be farmed. But, sadly over time, it was discovered that this muck actually lacked many of the nutrients needed to grow most crops; however, farmers soon learned the application of nitrogen and phosphorus transformed the muck into the perfect medium for growing crops. But, it wasn't until after 1959's U.S. embargo of Cuban agricultural products, and sugar in particular, that growing sugarcane became the dominant farming enterprise in South Florida, leading eventually to today's situation where almost every acre of land south of the lake is owned by large sugar producers.

Benjamin next took time to describe the farming methodology required to grow sugarcane, noting, while cane will certainly grow in the muck of the Everglades, that area is not really an ideal environment for it to flourish since sugarcane cultivation requires that a stable water table be maintained at a depth of about twenty inches under the cane. The problem in the Glades is that the natural water table is about two feet on top of the underlying muck. That problem had primarily been dealt with by the draining of the swamp.

A more serious issue was Florida's natural wet/dry seasonal cycles, in which almost all of the area's rain falls during the summer months, a problem for farmers which necessitated the active cooperation of the U.S. Army Corps of Engineers either to pump water onto fields during the dry months or pump water from the fields, either into the lake or into the Glades, during the monsoonal months. Water, of course, that was untreated and full of phosphorus and other harmful pollutants, which then flowed either out of the lake, into the estuaries on both sides of the state, or into the portions of the Everglades that were not being farmed.

This pollution, according to Benjamin, was a primary culprit in the destruction of our coasts' pristine waters, and served as a catalyst for our area's increasingly common outbreaks of red tide, a salt water algae bloom responsible for massive fish kills. I noted, as he warmed to his subject, low murmurs of approval from various tables around the room, punctuated by occasional louder interjections of support. I also noticed Commissioner Powell beginning to look increasingly uncomfortable.

Benjamin, possibly noting the Commissioner's discomfort, shifted his subject to praising efforts that certain local politicians had made over the past decades to address our water quality issues. He specifically noted laws that had phased out the widespread use of septic tanks, efforts that forced the use of reclaimed water for irrigation, laws that banned the application of fertilizer during the rainy season, and especially, the program that purchased threatened watershed areas in order to use them to help store and filter storm water run-off.

After he described these praiseworthy efforts, he specifically recognized and thanked Commissioner Thunderburke for having played a leading role in their implementation. The crowd enthusiastically gave that commissioner a round of applause. As the applause swelled I noticed the face of the other commissioner in attendance had reddened. Whether from anger or embarrassment, I couldn't tell.

When the applause died the speaker returned to the subject of the damage done to the area's waters by the sugar industry. He displayed several slides that effectively quantified the extent of the damage done, then discussed what he believed to be the source of the problems—the sugar fields south of the lake.

He introduced a plan that he felt would be the solution to all of the water problems plaguing the region. This plan, a portion of the broader Comprehensive Everglades Restoration Program, he called Everglades Project Six. It called for the purchase of fifty thousand acres of sugar land south of the lake to create a flow way that would convey water from the lake to the Everglades, thereby alleviating the massive discharge of polluted water into the estuaries of South Florida. He went on to suggest the cost of this acquisition could easily be paid for by simply repealing the thirty million annual payments that Lee County makes to the Southwest Florida Water Management District for the maintenance of the canals that run throughout the sugarcane fields.

By this time he had some in the crowd applauding. Soon the low murmurs of approval had swelled into exultant cheers, as the program chairwoman leaped to her feet to lead a chant of, "Project Six is the fix! Project Six is the fix!"

Sensing there was nothing more he could do to ramp the crowd's enthusiasm to a higher level, Benjamin opened the presentation to questions. I noticed the first hand in the air was Frank Osceola's, but the speaker seemed to ignore him intentionally, recognizing instead the waving hand of the attractive lady who had assisted in setting up the projection screen.

She asked, "What should the average citizen do to support making sure this outcome happens?"

While it was a reasonable enough question, I couldn't help but believe it had been pre-planned because Benjamin immediately specified, with the help of the next several PowerPoint pages, steps that citizens could take and legislation they should support. He also mentioned one of the most important things would be to vote for candidates who would support these types of initiatives. As he did I noticed he turned toward the commissioners standing near the door. When he turned back to face the crowd, I noticed an obvious twinkle in his eye.

He continued to take questions, all the while ignoring Skunkfoot's attempts to be recognized. Then he said he would like to close with a special announcement. After allowing a suitable period for suspense to build, he continued, "Those of you who have followed this issue know that I have long argued for the implementation of Project Six. So long, in fact, that I had almost given up believing, despite my public statements to the contrary, that its adoption would ever happen, but tonight I want you to know that I am now more optimistic than I have ever been because, while it is far from being approved, I believe that an announcement from the Governor's office to implement Project Six is imminent. I asked Commissioners Thunderburke and Powell to be with us tonight since they have both indicated to me privately that, if this proposal is made by the Governor, they will support it. "

With that the room erupted in enthusiastic applause. That, I'm sure, the speaker had expected. But I'd bet he had not expected the loud voice that rang out from the back of the room.

"You filthy, double-crossing bastard!" It was Frank Osceola shouting at Jay Benjamin.

"How dare you? What gives you the right to pollute the Everglades? How could you think it's good to pump billions of gallons of tainted water into God's sanctuary? If sugar's pollution is bad for the high-priced real estate of Sanibel and Palm Beach, why isn't it also bad for the Glades? The land you propose as your solution is the hallowed home of my people. It was our last refuge as we evaded the final desperate attempts of the whites to remove us to the West. It's land consecrated by the blood and tears of my ancestors. Once, all of Florida was our home, but now, what you propose to flood with filth, is all that we have left. If you inundate the Everglades with your contamination, our sacred home will be destroyed, and that will be the final chapter in the long, painful war of destruction that people like you have waged against my people! Jay Benjamin, I want you to know that if an agreement to flood our holy home with the filth and poisons of your people is implemented, I will hold you personally responsible. And if you allow this to happen, the spirits of my ancestors will place a curse on you and your soul, and I can assure you that, if they do, you will never live to see your pollution desecrate our lands." With that Frank turned and calmly walked out the back door. Amidst the ensuing uproar I noticed the two Commissioners had also left the building. For a moment the crowd was stunned. Jay Benjamin was clearly taken back by the vehemence of this attack, and his complexion was pale. But, shortly he was surrounded by supporters who looked as if they were doing their best to assure him that Frank was just a Pine Island nutcase whom shouldn't be taken seriously. I left as soon as I could, reflecting as I did that the evening's meeting had more than lived up to my expectations

.

Chapter Six

I had only been home a few minutes when Jill returned from her evening of canasta. She had obviously enjoyed a great evening and couldn't wait to share the night's gossip with me. Likewise, I couldn't wait to tell her about what occurred at my meeting, but being the experienced husband I am, I allowed her to go first.

"You won't believe what I learned tonight," she said. "Wasn't Jay Benjamin your speaker?"

"Yeah, he was," I answered. "And he did a great job."

"Well, from what I heard tonight from Georgia, he may not be as great a guy as you think."

"Go ahead. Bust my bubble. What did Georgia tell you?"

"You know that she and Robert like to go to the Seminole casino in Hollywood for date weekends. They don't so much like to gamble, but they say the restaurant and hotel are first class, and it's a good place to get away. Well, when I told her that Jay Benjamin was going to speak tonight, she told me that she and Robert were having dinner in the restaurant last week when they noticed Jay Benjamin also there. But, here's the good part, he wasn't alone. He and Amanda Johnson were sharing a booth in a dark corner, and according to Georgia, they were having a very, *very* lovely evening, if you know what I mean!"

"No. I don't know what you mean," I said.

"No. You wouldn't!"

"And?" I asked. "Who the heck is Amanda Johnson? Am I supposed to know her?"

"I think you know her," Jill answered. "She's the attractive blonde that attends the Pine Island Improvement Association meetings. You know, the one that you're so infatuated with. She's also a member of the Hookers, so I know her from there. She's married to Jerry Johnson. I know that he's loaded, but he must be at least seventy-five years old."

With that, she paused to gauge my reaction and give me time to present my defense, which I indignantly attempted to do, trying to assure her that I had no idea who Amanda Johnson was. She laughed and pointed out that my blush was all the evidence she needed.

Then she added, "Oh, you don't have to worry. She's not really your type, but you know who she is, alright. She's the woman who's so focused on what's happening to Matlacha's Back Bay."

"Oh, her!" I exclaimed, sensing an opening to get back to the news of the evening and refocus Jill's attention away from me. "So why were she and Jay Benjamin having dinner at the casino?" I asked.

"Well, according to Georgia, it didn't look like they were there to analyze water samples, but she did say they enjoyed several drinks, shared a bottle of Dom, finished dinner, and before they stumbled to the hotel's elevators, engaged in some pretty serious exploration of certain of her bodily zones. So maybe actually it was some type of fact-finding mission!"

"Wow!" I exclaimed. "I guess that explains that."

"What do you mean?" Jill asked.

"Well, it did look like they knew each other."

"Yeah," Jill laughed. "I think they might. So how did the meeting go?"

"Well," I replied. "It was actually a great presentation, and I think almost everyone enjoyed it. At least they did up until when Frank Osceola threatened to kill Jay Benjamin."

"He what?!" Jill exclaimed. "He actually threatened to murder Jay Benjamin?"

"Well, he didn't actually say that, but he did threaten to place a curse on him, and I think Benjamin took it seriously."

"Well, he damn well should," she replied. "Those Seminole curses are not something to be taken lightly. You've heard about the President's Curse, haven't you?"

"No. But what's unusual about cursing the President? Everybody does that at one time or another."

"Shut up, Jim, and you might learn something. This goes back to when Andrew Jackson was in office. In retaliation for the mayhem that he had unleashed on the Seminoles, Osceola, a chief of the Seminoles, proclaimed an eternal oath of war and destruction upon the U.S. and its presidents, and he directed the tribe's medicine man to decree that every future president elected in a year ending in zero would either be assassinated, be seriously injured, or die while in office."

"Oh, come on, Jill. That's just nonsense, and you know it."

"Jim, let me remind you about what you used to tell the kids: 'Your ears don't work when your mouth is open.' Now, close yours, and listen for a minute."

She continued, "Jackson always hated the American Indians, it didn't matter what tribe. In his opinion the only good 'Indian' was a dead 'Indian.' And, as a young man in the military he did his best to put that creed into effect. Then, once he was elected President, he decided to finally address the 'Indian Problem' by removing all of them—Cherokee, Creek, Choctaw, Chickasaw, and Seminole—to the West. To do that, he got Congress to approve the Indian Removal Act of 1830 and implemented it."

For a moment I thought about yawning and pretending to be bored, but something about the look in her eyes convinced me that such a move would not be wise. I refocused on what she was saying.

"Of course," she laughed, "this did not prove to be as easy as Jackson had envisioned, and this effort, among other things, led to the start of the Second Seminole War, which is where Chief Osceola came in. He refused to agree to the transfer and led his people in an armed uprising against the U.S. His forces were successful on the battle field, but in what was probably our country's most disreputable act in its history, when he came in to negotiate under the protection of the Army's white flag of truce they arrested him and took him to the stockade in St. Augustine. Is it any wonder that, to this day, the Seminoles don't trust the U.S.? But I digress. After the curse was put into effect, there have been eight U.S. Presidents who have either died in office, or who were seriously injured while in office, and all of their terms were associated with years ending in '0.'"

CHAPTER SIX

"Oh, come on, Jill, that's a bunch of crap, and you know it."

"Look it up, big guy," she said. "But I can tell you that you'll find Harrison, Taylor, Lincoln, Garfield, McKinley, Harding, Roosevelt, Kennedy, and Reagan were all done in or harmed by Osceola's curse."

"Yeah, well what about George W. Bush?" I asked. "Wasn't he elected in 2000? Last I heard he served two full terms, and he's still kicking."

"I can't answer that," she said. "Who knows? Maybe the curse has run its course, or maybe Osceola's ghost didn't think he was a real president. But, I'll tell you this, I wouldn't want to have a Seminole Curse put on me. That's for sure."

"Oh, come on. You're not really superstitious are you?"

"This is not about superstitions. This stuff is for real. You've been to Spook Hill in Lake Wales, haven't you?"

I think she could tell that she had gotten my attention with her reference to one our state's most amazing locations—a place that is reported to be haunted by the ghost of a Seminole Chief who had battled to the death on that spot with a gigantic alligator—a fight that resulted in the creation of a lake at the bottom of the hill. To this day that spirit allows vehicles that park in neutral at the bottom of that hill to roll without power all the way up to its top, and causes vehicles that park at its top to not be able to coast down that hill.

I knew that she'd made her point—I've been to Spook Hill many times.

Chapter Seven

The next several weeks passed quietly, but the weather was beautiful and the fishing was great. Late spring is the time when the migrations of many different species of fish and other creatures come by the shores of Southwest Florida. As our waters warm, manatee return to our estuaries and bait fish fill the Sound. And, of course, close behind the bait, you can find massive quantities of game fish. One of the first species to swim north is Spanish mackerel. Kenny and I love to fish for these, so I wasn't surprised when he called.

"Jim, I'm going to go out in the morning to troll for some Spanish. You want to go?"

"Of course I do. What time?"

"It looks like we'll have a good tide in the morning and the winds should be okay early. How does eight o'clock sound to you?"

"Perfect! See you in the morning."

With that I went downstairs to check on the rods I keep rigged for mackerel. These fish are voracious predators, prowling the bars at the mouth of the bay. This time of year the most effective method of fishing for them is to troll silver spoons. Mackerel have sharp teeth so it is critical that you use a strong leader to secure the lure to your line. In fact, many folks who troll for mackerel will tell you that you must use a wire leader for this purpose. But Kenny and I have found that fifty-pound fluorocarbon works even better. We believe that's because it's less visible to the fish and, as long as you periodically check to ensure the leader's not frayed, you won't have any more cut-offs than with wire.

We like to troll for mackerel using silver spoons. Of course, the lures are not actually spoons. But they are called that because many years ago anglers learned they could attach fish hooks to tea spoons, drag them through the water, and catch fish. The shape of the spoon as it passed through the water caused the lure to oscil-late and effectively imitated the swimming motion of nervous bait. Today, the household flatware is safe but that name is still used to describe this specific class of lure, and for this purpose they can be deadly.

Through trial and error we've learned to catch mackerel you need to troll at a speed just slightly faster than five knots. If you troll slower the spoon will sink and you'll likely end up catching blues—a less desirable species; faster, and the spoon will bounce along the surface, likely enticing more seagulls than fish.

The next morning I was waiting on my dock, rods in hand, as Kenny eased his boat alongside. He helped load my gear and a minute later we were underway. He has a deck boat (sometimes called a fancy pontoon boat). They are often perceived as being only good for partying, but Kenny has disproven that theory. His is a very effective fishing machine. Granted its large top can interfere with casting, but that inconvenience is more than made up for by the ample shade it provides. The vessel's shallow draft allows Kenny to prowl the skinny water near the mangroves where reds and snook like to hide.

Today shallow water was not our concern. Our plan was to troll along the long sand bar that runs south from the lower tip of Sanibel Island and extends across much of the mouth of San Carlos Bay. The water depth over this bar is about eight feet, and this area is a favorite haunt of hungry schools of Spanish mackerel.

Our lines were in the water by eight-thirty, and at eight-thirty-nine we had our first fish on board. You've got to love it when a plan comes together. By nine o'clock, we'd put five large mackerel in the cooler, and we had to take a break to catch our breath.

"Damn, Jim!" Kenny exclaimed. "Look at the deck. It looks like the floor of a slaughter house."

"You're right about that," I replied. "Those things sure bleed a lot."

"Yeah. Let me get a bucket and let's wash the deck off before it starts to dry. If I don't keep it clean, Janice will never let me hear the end of it."

"I hear you," I answered. "That kind of reminds me of what happened to Terry and Patti. Did you ever hear that story?"

"No. Can't say that I did. You're talking about Terry that helped us out up on Little Bokeelia?"

"The same. You know, of course, that he's a big hunter and fisherman—a Florida Cracker of the first degree. Well, one of the things he likes to do is to cast net for mullet so he can put them in his smoker. And, I've got to tell you, his smoked mullet dip is to die for. But, anyway, one day his boat was at the marina being worked on, so he thought he'd just take Patti's boat out to throw his net."

At this point, I couldn't help myself and started to laugh out loud. Kenny gave me a quizzical look.

"Excuse me, Kenny, but this story just cracks me up every time I think about it. You know how dirty a boat can get when you're throwing a net, so it wasn't long before Patti's boat was filthy from stem to stern: mud, mullet shit, blood, grass, you name it. And it smelled, too. When he'd caught all the fish he needed, he decided it'd be best to bring the boat back to the dock and use a water hose to clean it there. And that would have worked out fine, but unfortunately Patti was waiting at the dock when he pulled up."

At this point I started to laugh again. Then, with tears running down my face, I continued.

"Apparently, she has a thing about her boat being absolutely spotless. So, needless to say, when she saw the condition it was in, she wasn't happy. To hear Terry tell it, it was quite a scene. Long story short, he had to spend the better part of two days cleaning and disinfecting the boat to get it back to Patti's standards. I think he used a whole gallon of bleach, and who knows what else, to make that boat shine. And, to this day, she won't let Terry set foot on her boat."

"Dang, Jim! That's nothing. Did I ever tell you about the time I used my sister-in-law's car to go buy some shrimp?"

"No, Kenny, I don't think so."

"I didn't think so since I'm kind of embarrassed about what happened. And what makes it so bad is that all I was trying to do was be helpful to my sister-in-law. Well, anyway, you know how crazy Gigi is about keeping her car clean. Well, she'd gone out of town for a couple of weeks, and she'd asked me to drive it just to keep the battery charged. And, believe me, I was extra careful to not get it dirty when I drove it up to Matlacha to D&D's Bait Shop to buy a couple dozen of those nice jumbo shrimp."

At this point I interrupted Kenny. "You don't mean those things we fish for redfish with? Those things are almost as big as lobsters!"

"Yeah, Jim, that's exactly what I drove up there to buy. I had them put the shrimp in a five-gallon bucket and set that on the floor board in front of the passenger side seat. And I was extra careful driving all the way home just to make sure not even a single drop of water sloshed out of that bucket. When I got home I took the bucket out, locked her car in the driveway, and went fishing. Jim, I thought I'd done good."

"Ok, Kenny," I asked. "What happened?"

"Well, when Gigi got back about a week later, she went out to drive her car somewhere, and as soon as she opened the car's door, the smell of something rotten just about floored her. She came back in the house and headed straight for me. Let me tell you, she was more than just a trifle pissed. I'd never ever seen her that mad. I, of course, proclaimed my innocence, knowing that I'd been very careful with her car, and had kept it locked other than that one time I drove it. But being the good brother-in-law that I am, I went out to check to see what she was talking about. I expected maybe a little smell of mold or something like that. But,

THE SILVER SPOON MURDER

I've got to tell you, I was wrong and she was right! Something had certainly died and decayed in her car. But, for the life of me, I couldn't figure out what had happened. I looked that car over inside and out: I looked in the trunk; I looked underneath it; I looked in the engine compartment; I looked everywhere, but I couldn't find a damn thing. Finally, after about an hour of searching, I shined a flashlight way up under the front passenger seat, and I figured out what happened. It seems that a couple of those jumbos had somehow jumped out of that five gallon bucket, flopped up under the seat, and died. Now, I've got to tell you, if you put dead shrimp in a locked car in the hot Florida sun and let it sit for a week, you won't believe just how bad the smell will be! It'll make you gag."

By this point I was laughing so hard I was about to fall out of the boat. But Kenny continued.

"Jim, damn it, it really wasn't that funny. Needless to say, my ass was in big trouble, and I spent the whole next week trying to get that smell out of her car. I bet I spent a hundred dollars on disinfectants and deodorizers. But nothing worked until I found a car detailer over in the Cape who knew how to deal with the problem. That cost me another two hundred dollars, but that finally worked, and Gigi could once again drive her car. But not me. I don't think she'll ever loan me her keys again."

"Damn, Kenny! I don't blame her. And I'm not going to let you drive my car either."

With that, we returned to fishing. By eleven o'clock we had our limit, and were on the way home. Another great day of fishing the waters of Southwest Florida.

Chapter Eight

That night I finally got around to reading the morning's news-paper. I know that having to read the day's paper is a habit that clearly identifies me as a technological Neanderthal, but somehow my day just doesn't feel complete unless I've done that. Honestly, for me, pushing buttons while staring at a screen of pulsating pixels just doesn't provide the same fix. It'll do in a pinch, but somehow it just doesn't provide the same type of reward that I can get by sitting back in a comfortable chair, turning large sheets of newsprint, and contemplating, at my own pace, the mean-ing of the words printed on them. And don't get me started on videos—God, how I hate them. By the time one actually loads on my iPad I can have already read a whole section of the paper. So don't cancel my subscription to the 'News Press' just yet.

Today's paper was particularly interesting. I always make a point of reading the Editorial page and the accompanying Letters to the Editor section. Frequently I'm inspired by the fervor those letter-writers craft into their replies about subjects that are obviously near to their hearts. Good for them. That kind of passion is critical to our democracy, but one of today's letters was especially interesting; not so much for its zeal, as for its unexpected guidance.

It was written by the recent speaker at the Pine Island Improvement Association, Jay Benjamin, so, of course, I was interested, but I had to do a double-take when I saw the headline: "Benjamin Slams Everglades Deal!" Given the enthusiasm for this agreement he had displayed at that meeting, this attitude was not at all what I would have expected. I read further, and by the time I had finished, all I could do was shake my head.

The correspondence began with him detailing his views on the many benefits of the Project Six solution to the area's water quality issues, but what followed was Benjamin's advice to readers, urging them to voice their opposition to the Governor's soon-to-be-announced agreement to implement this measure. Benjamin's letter explained his opposition was not because he had lost faith in this fix's benefits, but rather because he had learned from sources he considered to be unimpeachable, that the Governor, both political parties, and Big Sugar, in crafting this soon-to-be-announced agreement had engaged in one of the most extreme cases of corruption in the state's long history of political sleaze. Without going into the specifics, he outlined the structure of a deal that involved the State of Florida agreeing to grant to various key owners of Florida's sugar industry monopoly rights for full casino gambling in Broward and Dade Counties. In exchange, these owners would agree to sell to the state, at what Benjamin believed was a vastly inflated price, one hundred thousand acres of sugar land.

Benjamin claimed that, in essence, this deal not only gave away the rights to what was potentially the most lucrative gambling franchise in the country, but also provided the funds necessary for the owners of sugar to build the casinos and hotels necessary to capitalize on it. For having arranged this deal, Benjamin claimed the Governor and supporting politicians on both sides of the aisle would never again have to beg for campaign funds, or for any other kind of funds as far as that goes. The final sections of his letter noted how disappointed he was to have to oppose something to which he had devoted so much of his life, and made a promise he would continue to look into this matter and would disclose, as he could, the specific evidence and names of all those involved.

"Jill," I shouted. "Did you read the letter in the paper from Jay Benjamin?"

"No," she replied without a lot of enthusiasm. "I must have missed that. Was it interesting?"

"You've got to read this," I said, giving her the paper and emphatically pointing to the article.

She spent a minute with it, then with a puzzled expression on her face, said, "That's surprising. I wonder what this is really about? Maybe he's more concerned about that curse than you think."

"Yeah, right!" I said. "You know that I don't believe in that crap, but I'll tell you this, I sure as heck do believe in the ability of our public officials to amaze us with their willingness to defraud and deceive."

You're right about that," Jill responded. "There's never a dull moment around here!"

"Well, I've got a bad feeling that it's about to get a lot more exciting. I just hope that this time trouble stays off our island. We've certainly had more than our share."

Jill gave me her raised-eyebrow look. It was a look that I interpreted as conveying a silent warning to keep my nose out of the middle of anything that had to do with trouble, but, at the same time, I thought it was a look that managed to convey more than just a little worry.

I gave her wink in reply and then asked what was for dinner.

As she turned and walked away, I thought I might have heard her mumble something about someone being a jerk, but I reasoned it would probably not have been in my best interest to explore that particular subject any further.

Chapter Nine

Several days later, I was sitting in a chair on our pool deck. I had put a couple of tarpon reels on the table, oiling them to ensure they would be ready for the upcoming season. I'd just finished tightening the last screw when I overheard Jill talking loudly on the upstairs phone.

A couple of minutes later she banged opened the French doors that overlooked the pool and started to scream and cry. I couldn't completely make out what she was saying, but I thought I could make out: "Frank… arrested… murder… awful… the girls said… and do something!"

"Whoa!" I exclaimed. "Wait a minute. I'll be right there."

I ran inside. "Now," I commanded. "Slow down and start over. But, first, take a deep breath. Now, tell me what's going on."

"Oh, Jim," she began. "I'm sorry, but it's just awful. That was Georgia on the phone. She'd just been talking with Roxy, who'd just heard from Carolyn, who'd heard from Delmar, who'd heard from somebody at Ragged Ass that Frank Osceola had been arrested by the Sherriff's Office this morning for Jay Benjamin's murder. The girls want you to do something to help Frank, and I do, too. And we want you to do it now! Frank's a good friend of Georgia and Robert, and she doesn't think he would hurt a fly, and neither do any of us, and you need to talk to Lieutenant Collins and get him to release Frank. Please!"

"Jill, calm down. You know I can't do something like that. That's just not how things work. If they arrested Frank, then they must have had a real good reason to think he was involved. But did you say that Jay Benjamin had been murdered?"

"That's what Georgia said. She heard it from Roxy, who—"

"I know," I interrupted her. "She heard it from Carolyn, who heard it from Delmar, who'd heard it from somebody who was having breakfast at Ragged Ass. So how was Jay Benjamin killed?"

"They didn't know that, but they said his body had been found over on Captiva in one of Frank's trash bins. I guess that's why they arrested him."

"That and the fact the whole town heard him threaten to kill Jay Benjamin!" I agreed.

"But that was just a threat to put a curse on him, not a threat to actually kill him," Jill protested. "And, besides, that was only if Jay got Project Six implemented. You saw the article in the paper, he was lobbying against it."

"But it still looks as if the proposal is going to be implemented. The Governor has indicated he supports it, and from what I've read, the House and Senate are behind it, too. I think it's a done deal. Maybe that was enough for Frank, or enough for one of his relatives."

"Jim, you can't really believe that Frank Osceola would actually kill someone. I know he sometimes comes across kind of rough but, according to Georgia, he's one of the sweetest guys she's ever met. She says he wouldn't hurt a fly. There's got to be something you can do. Will you at least call Mike Collins and try to find out what's going on?"

"Look, Jill, I'm not going to get in the middle of this. I've already almost been killed twice since we moved here. Both times I was just trying to help a friend, a friend who *was* in the middle of something like this. But those were *friends*. We don't even really know Frank that well. There's no good reason for me to get involved in this."

Jill gave me her best 'I'm hurt' look, the one where her jaw protrudes and begins to quiver, her lips pout, and her eyes moisten. Then she asked, "But what about the girls? Aren't they our friends?"

"Oh, shit!" I mumbled to myself, recognizing the futility of further resistance. "I'll call Mike."

Chapter Ten

Lieutenant Mike Collins is a Chief Investigator for the Lee County Sherriff's Department with specific responsibility for Lee County's northern Gulf islands. His territory includes Sanibel, Capitva, North Captiva, and Pine Island; essentially anything that touches Pine Island Sound. I had gotten to know him when he led the investigations into the two other murders that had recently occurred in our town, murders of people we knew and cared about. From those interactions I knew that Collins was a competent and honest officer. I liked him, respected the way he went about his job, and knew that he could be trusted to do what was right.

On the other hand, I wasn't sure he would have ever solved the mysteries of who had killed our friends if not for several of us on the island, despite his instructions to the contrary, having gotten involved in the investigations. At the very least, it would have taken him a lot longer. While I'm sure he didn't appreciate that a group of bungling retirees had played important roles in ultimately bringing the killers to justice, we had gone out of the way to keep our contributions out of the public eye, and had done everything we could to ensure that Collins had gotten credit for solving the crimes. From what I'd seen on the news and read in the paper, he and his boss, Sheriff Sam Brown, had enjoyed the intense, if short-lived glow of public praise for a job well-done. We hadn't talked since then. I dialed his cell, hoping for a cordial response. I should have known better.

"Oh, my God! Just when I thought that my day couldn't get any worse. Please, Dear Lord, I beg you, take pity on my long-suffering soul and save me from investigational interference by Pine Island's Over the Hill Gang in the most important case of my miserable, poorly compensated, but diligently pursued, underappreciated public service career. Jim Story, make my day and tell me that this is just a social call."

"Michael! It's good to hear from you, too. But I am so disappointed you would think that I would ever again interfere in any official investigation of yours. Trust me. I've learned my lesson."

"That's good to hear. How's Jill?"

"She's great. But, honestly, she *is* why I'm calling?"

"Uh, oh. What'd she do? Get caught speeding on Stringfellow again?"

"She's fine. And I'd be the last to know if your guys gave her a citation. But please don't get upset with me because she *did* ask me to call you about Frank Osceola. She and her girlfriends want you to know they don't believe he killed Jay Benjamin."

"Well, Christ, Jim. Why didn't you say so earlier! Given that piece of critical new evidence, I'll turn him loose right now! If Jill and the girls think he's innocent, then, without question, he must be. I'll ignore the fact that half of the residents of Pine Island and two county commissioners recently heard him in a public meeting threaten to kill Benjamin. I'll ignore the fact that we found the victim buried in the bottom of one of his dumpsters. I'll overlook the victim was killed after being struck on the back of the head by a shark club that matches one we found in its rack on the Indian's barge. I'll ignore that said bat had microscopic traces of Benjamin's blood and tissue still on it, despite the Chief having apparently made an attempt to wipe it clean. And I won't pay any attention that my suspect has no alibi for his whereabouts on last Thursday evening, the night when Jay Benjamin was sent to meet his maker. All of that be damned, I'll just take Jill's word for it."

At that point, he went silent and I knew he had left the ball sitting in the middle of my court. You would think at my age I would have learned to just let it lie and keep my mouth shut. Who knows? Maybe it's early onset dementia. I just couldn't help myself.

"Mike, I know you can't do that, so I'd appreciate it if you'd stop insulting me with your station house sarcasms. If you've got proof, you've got proof. But I would point out there are a lot of other folks around this area who have had problems with Jay Benjamin. Maybe someone else had a reason to do him in."

"So, Sherlock, just who do you think might have bashed our ex-County Commissioner in the head with Frank Osceola's shark bat other than Frank Osceola?"

"Maybe it was another member of one of the tribes. I know many of them are concerned about Project Six. And what about any number of local developers whose projects he's managed to ax over the years? And we all know that Benjamin had been doing his best to publicly embarrass the newly elected Commissioner who took his seat. I was at a meeting where that guy looked mad enough to kill Benjamin with his bare hands. And I'm sure you saw the victim's recent letter in the newspaper? He accused the Governor, most of the politicians in the state, and the owners of Big Sugar of a massive political corruption scheme and threatened to expose them further. To me, that sounds like more than enough reason to kill somebody. And, beyond that, I know for a fact that he's been messing around with the wife of a fellow up in Matlacha. You want that guy's name, I'll give it to you. So from where I sit, it looks like there's a whole list of folks out there, besides Frank Osceola, who might have wanted to kill the guy."

"You have any evidence?"

"No."

"Give my best to Jill and the girls." Click.

Chapter Eleven

The exchange with Mike Collins soured my disposition. It would probably be more accurate to say the exchange further soured my disposition since I was already irritated from having recognized a few days earlier my dock needed to be stained—again! Only two years ago I had spent several days cleaning and painting it and had assumed that it would be good for at least five years before it need to be treated again. But I had failed to consider the impact sun, humidity, and salt have on structures down here; that, and the fact that I had purchased the cheapest grade of barn stain available at our local big box hardware store. That selection had proven to be a mistake, one I was determined not to make again. This time I had carefully done my research and had found a product manufactured in Ft. Myers that claimed to have been specifically formulated for Florida's climate.

Jill was up-island having her hair touched up. She's made friends with a nice lady who not only does hair, but also performs manicures and pedicures out of her home. Not only that, and this may be hard for someone not on the island to believe, but she also raises chickens in her back yard. Jill always tries to bring back a dozen freshly laid organic eggs. I'm glad she does because those eggs taste so much better than what you can buy in the store.

Because the hairdresser has a couple of young kids in the house, I understood that Jill would be gone for at least three, maybe four hours. Given that, I decided to tackle the first phase of my dock's restoration. I knew if all went well, this project would take four days. The first to strip off the old stain; the next, to neutralize and brighten the bare wood; then a couple more to apply two coats of new stain. Four days if it didn't rain and if all else went well. But I recognized my projects rarely proceed exactly as planned. I had looked into having someone do the project, but that bid had come back at twelve hundred dollars: three hundred for materials, and the rest for labor. Now that I am retired I had quickly reasoned my time was worth a lot less than that.

I had just applied the first coat of stripper when I saw Kenny heading out of the canal in his deck boat. I stopped what I was doing and motioned him over. He eased against the pilings and looped a line around one of them, holding on to the bitter end.

"Jim, what the heck are you doing to your dock?" he asked.

"What's it look like I'm doing? I'm stripping it so I can re-stain it."

"Didn't you just do that?" Kenny asked.

"Yeah. But look at it. It looks like crap. I can't stand it. You going fishing?"

"Yep. I'm going to hop down to the big bayou and try to fool a red into sucking down a jumbo shrimp. You want to go?"

"I'd love to but I'm in the middle of this now. Besides I wouldn't be much fun. I'm trying to work off the negative energy I got when I spoke to Mike Collins this morning."

"So you did give him a call? Janice told me Jill said you were going to try to get him to let Frank out. I'm guessing from your disposition that call wasn't successful?"

I laughed. "Well, he's not planning to spring Frank any time soon, if that's what you mean."

Kenny smiled and said, "I didn't expect him to. But did you learn anything interesting?"

I told him what Lieutenant Collins had said about the evidence against Frank.

"Well," Kenny responded. "That's something, alright. But I know Frank and I don't think he'd do something like this. For whatever that's worth."

"Why not?" I asked.

"Oh, I don't know. We drink a lot of beer together down at Froggy's and I've seen him pretty stewed, but I've never seen him try to fight or anything like that. He's always kind of been the peace-maker in the bar. And, besides, now that I know Benjamin was killed on Thursday night, I think Frank has an alibi."

"Really! Well, why in the hell hasn't he told Collins about this? If he has an alibi there's no way they can hold him," I said.

"He probably won't tell him," Kenny replied.

I opened my mouth to respond, but before I could get my question out, Kenny continued.

"I'm pretty sure Frank was with a woman that night. But I'd bet that he won't admit it, and she sure as hell ain't going to come forward."

"Married, huh?" I asked.

"Happily," Kenny replied.

"Shit. Kenny, do you know who the woman was?"

"Yep. But I can't tell you, I can't tell Janice, I can't tell anybody. But now I'm sure it wasn't Frank that whacked Jay Benjamin."

"You got any ideas who did it?" I asked.

"I don't have a clue. But it wasn't Frank. And, by the way, you didn't hear this from me. Now I'm going fishing. Good luck with your dock."

With that, Kenny unlooped the line, pushed his boat back into the canal, and headed toward the bayou.

Chapter Twelve

I spent the rest of the day scrubbing and pressure washing the dock. One thing I've learned since I've retired in Southwest Florida is the most important piece of equipment that homeowners here need is a good pressure washer. Mold, mildew, and other assorted quickly accumulating types of grunge make this investment a necessity. Initially, I had made the mistake of buying the cheapest one I could find at the Depot, but it hadn't taken me long to upgrade. Today I had put this machine to a tough stain-stripping test, a test it was passing with flying colors.

I took a break for lunch about noon and was inside when Kenny returned from his fishing expedition. I knew he had returned because, as was his custom, he honked the horn on his boat when he passed just to say hello. I knew that he'd been successful fishing. He'd texted me earlier a picture of him holding a nice thirty-inch red. I suspected that he and the ladies in his house would be enjoying a dinner tonight of baked freshly caught fish.

Jill came home mid-afternoon. Her hair looked great and she had a dozen delicious-looking brown eggs in hand as she walked down to the dock to see how I was progressing. Since I was soaked in layers of perspiration we couldn't embrace, but I did welcome her with my most alluring wink; at least I had hoped it was an alluring wink, but I suspect she may have just thought I had sweat in my eye.

"Jim, the dock's looking good. I was worried when I heard that you were planning to do this project by yourself. But I've got to say, so far, I'm impressed. You might actually pull this one off."

"Thanks, babe, I think. I see you've got some eggs. How're Paula and the kids?"

"They're good," Jill responded. "Of course, it's always a little bit of a mad house around there, but I really love her kids. They're so sweet."

"Jill, while you're here, let me ask you a question. Do you know if any of your friends has been sleeping with Frank Osceola?"

Jill laughed. "My friends! You've got to be kidding. Why would you ask something silly like that?"

I told her what Kenny had told me.

"Wow. I wonder who that might be? You want me to ask the girls to see if they know?"

"No. Not yet. Later, if we really need to know, we can snoop some, but right now I think I need to let Mike Collins know. What do you think?"

"How'd your call go with him this morning?" she asked.

"Not too well." I filled her in. "You know I think I'll call him back and rattle his cage a little bit with this new piece of information. You know, just shake up his sense of certainty a little."

CHAPTER TWELVE

"Have fun," Jill said. "Oh, babe, by the way, I see a spot you missed over near the second piling."

By four o'clock, the dock was stain-free and I was looking forward to tackling the next phase of the project in the morning. But what I was looking forward to even more was getting cleaned up and then enjoying a tall, icy scotch and water or two. It's true that some days I do feel guilty about drinking. After we retired I'd quickly learned that since every day is Saturday, you needed to learn out how to limit your alcohol consumption. For the most part, I'd been able to do that, but given today's hard work, I felt that I'd earned a reward. Besides, I wanted to be properly lubricated when I made my call to the Sheriff's Department.

Lieutenant Collins answered on the fourth ring; I could tell he'd looked at the caller ID.

"What's the matter, Story? Jill make you call back and try again? Why don't you just have her call me directly? You know that I'd much rather talk with her than you."

"Mike, all that power the Sheriff's given you must be going to your head. I can't imagine any reason she'd want to talk to you."

"Whoa, big guy! You're getting a little testy, aren't you? You been drinking?"

"Of course I've been drinking! I am on the island and it *is* almost five o'clock. But that's beside the point. I heard something today that I think you ought to know. That is if that buzz-cut skull of yours isn't too thick to consider any alternatives to your open-and-shut case, railroad job against Frank Osceola that you've been working on."

"Damn, Jim—I never knew you were so sensitive. I must have hit a nerve this morning."

"Yeah. You must have. I guess I just expected a little warmer reception after all the help my buddies and I have given you. But I'm not calling looking for an apology. I've got something for you. But, first, Frank Osceola didn't threaten to kill Benjamin at the Improvement Association meeting; he threatened him with a curse. I was there; I know. This distinction probably doesn't mean a damn thing, but Mike, if you're going to tick me off, you at least ought to make sure your conviction speech is technically correct. But I did hear something today that might just be meaningful. It's not much, and I can't verify it, but I do think it's something you ought to know about."

"Shoot."

"You remember my friend Kenny?"

"Yeah. How can I forget him? Talkative little guy, loves his beer, and likes to stir things up. Seems like he's always in the middle of the shit whenever something's going down. He was up at Little Bokeelia with you, wasn't he?"

"Yep. That's him. Anyway, apparently, he and Frank are stool mates up at Froggy's. Kenny told me this morning that he has reason to believe that Frank was in the sack with a happily married island lady on the evening that Jay Benjamin met his demise."

"First I've heard of it. Wonder why Frank hasn't bothered to tell me this?"

"Scruples, I guess."

"That's all you've got?"

"That's all I've got. But, Mike, I told you this morning the girls don't think Frank killed Benjamin. And now I'm telling you, I don't think he did either. I'm sorry to be the bearer of bad news, but I'm afraid that you're going to have to get off your butt and actually conduct a real police investigation."

"Jim, I appreciate the information. And, Jim, one other thing. If y'all are planning to go out tonight, let Jill do the driving."

Chapter Thirteen

The next morning's newspaper contained several interesting articles: a front page article discussed the status of ongoing negotiations between the Governor and the Seminole Tribe of Florida concerning renewal of the tribe's expiring gambling rights. I knew those rights granted to the Tribe an exclusive franchise for gambling activities in all of the state's counties, excluding Dade and Broward. I had previously heard those negotiations were underway, but I had not realized until I read this article the Seminole Tribe had recently contributed one million dollars to the Governor's reelection fund. When I read that, I could only shake my head and question why someone, somewhere, wasn't raising a stink about this conflict of interest. I also had to wonder whether any of this might relate in some fashion to what had been disclosed in Jay Benjamin's letter to the newspaper.

Further along, in the local section of the paper, I discovered something else that made me question what was going on in Tallahassee. This article described the recent appointment to the

Board of Directors of the Southwest Florida Water Management District of Mitchell Thornberry, a fellow identified as being the CEO of the Royal Ranch's Florida Real Estate arm. I didn't really like the sound of that, but when I remembered having read a few weeks earlier about the Governor's recent deer hunting trip to the Royal Ranch in Texas, I liked it even less.

Finally, buried deep in the business section of the paper, listed among recent real estate transactions in Lee County, I noticed that a subsidiary of the Royal Ranch had purchased over the past month six separate tracts of land located on the northern end of Pine Island. While the largest of these purchases was only a little over four hundred acres, when added together they totaled almost three thousand acres—a huge tract by Pine Island standards. I couldn't be sure but I suspected that this cumulative parcel stretched from one shoreline of the island to the other. I was pleased to note this land was all zoned for agricultural use, but that made me wonder if the Royal Ranch had suddenly developed an interest in growing mangoes or raising palm trees. After a little thought I concluded that starting a new small-scale farming operation probably wasn't the real reason the Royal Ranch wanted property on our quiet tropical island.

All of this information aroused my curiosity. Despite having been raised in Florida, I realized I really didn't know that much about the sugar industry. Now, filling in that gap in my knowledge base seemed far more important than completing phase two of my dock restoration plan.

"Jill, I need to do some research on something. If you need me I'm going to be downstairs on the computer."

"You want me to call the dock guy back?" she asked.

"No, of course not. I'm going to finish the dock, but I think it'll be good to let it dry another day before I put the brightener on it." I was stretching the truth, but I thought my explanation sounded convincing.

Jill, as is her way, knew better.

"Jim, I know what you're doing. You've just got to learn more about what might have happened to Jay Benjamin, and if that will help Frank, I'm all for it. But, please, don't let this screw up the dock. If we need to call someone to finish it, let's do it. It's not that much money."

"Jill," I replied somewhat indignantly, "I'm going to finish the dock. But I think it'll be good to let it dry for a day or so."

"Whatever!" was her response.

Chapter Fourteen

My first query was for information on the Everglades. It didn't take long to discover that, contrary to what I'd always thought, the Everglades is not made up of one large stretch of swampland. Rather, the 'Glades,' which is generally thought of as including all of the land south of Lake Okeechobee, can be considered as having two distinct topographies. The area to the south and west of the lake is what is commonly referred to as the Big Cypress. Much of this area for most of the year is not a swamp at all. Other than during the rainy season, the land is relatively dry. The northern portion of this area supports large stands of pine forests. This is the home to deer, bear, and panthers, and historically, was where most of the Seminole lived. The southern portion is home to the nation's only remaining virgin growths of bald cypress. At the very south, the cypress gives way to mangroves as the land gradually transitions into the Ten Thousand Islands of Southwest Florida.

To the east and south of the lake between Big Cypress and the limestone ridges that run along the state's east coast is the famous River of Grass, the area that most think of when they think of the Everglades. Historically, this area, really a fifty-mile-wide, one hundred-mile-long slough, is the channel through which historically, during the rainy season, the lake would overflow and eventually make its way to the pristine shallows of Florida Bay, after being filtered by its slow meandering through a hundred miles of saw grass.

But now, due to a 1948 Act of Congress, the River of Grass has been divided into three zones from north to south. The northern most is referred to as the Everglades Agricultural Zone. This is where the muck upon which the saw grass would grow has been drained, and where sugarcane is now farmed. In ages past, this area would have been two feet under water during the rainy season, but now the water table is carefully maintained by the U.S. Army Corps of Engineers almost two feet beneath the surface of the land in order to create optimal conditions for sugarcane to grow.

That excess water has to go somewhere. Some of it gets pumped back into the lake. Some of it is pumped south into the second zone, the water conservation areas. As much as anything, these areas were designed to ensure that the populations living on Florida's east coast would always have fresh water to drink. To some extent the pumping of water into this area is meant to mimic the natural flow of water during the rainy season; what is not natural is the composition of the water that is pumped into this portion of the Glades. In ages past, when this area was the home of the Miccosukee, the level of phosphorus in the waters that flowed from the lake was extremely low, estimated to have been something less than ten parts per billion. But after the creation of the sugar farms; after the growth of the cattle industry along the Kissimmee River—a waterway channeled and straightened by the Corps of Engineers to dump unfiltered water directly into Okeechobee; and after Disney World, and the metropolitan sewage and runoff that resulted, that concentration of phosphorus increased to over five hundred parts per billion. Saw grass doesn't use phosphorus to grow; however, other plants, plants such as cat tail, thrive on it. Consequently, in the water conservation areas native saw grass has been completely squeezed out, replaced by dense growths of cat tail; growths of cat tail so thick that birds can't reach the water to feed. But even if they could they wouldn't find any fish to eat since the water itself is now almost completely devoid of dissolved oxygen.

The Miccosukee Tribe has been granted by settlement agreement with the State of Florida the perpetual right to use and enjoy this area. This agreement stated the land would be preserved in its natural state, would be maintained to preserve fresh water for aquatic life, wildlife, and their habitats, and would assure proper water management of water resources. These rights, however, were not absolute, being subject to the water management activities of the U.S. Army Corps of Engineers and the Southwest Florida Water Management District. The Tribe and our Government have been arguing in court about this agreement since.

The third zone, the area to the south of the water conservation areas, the area that nobody else wanted, is the area that eventually became the Everglades National Park. But, today, the park is but a shadow of its former self. Increasingly, it is nothing but parched earth, a land drying up due to lack of meaningful and consistent flows of fresh water. Farther south and west, beyond where the limestone coastal ridges end, lay Florida Bay and the Ten Thousand Islands. This is where the purified waters from the River of Grass once emptied, a critical element of what was once one of the world's most pristine marine environments, but no longer. Today, these areas, the coral reefs, and the grass flats are dying, being slowly killed by a lack of clean, fresh water.

After reading all of this I was, of course, depressed, but I was also angry to think our country had allowed, in fact, had caused this to happen, and possibly an entity known as Big Sugar was somehow largely to blame; an entity that may have also recently murdered a good man in Southwest Florida. I knew I had to learn more.

I decided to start with the basics. What is sugarcane and how does it grow? So that's what I queried next.

There was a ton of information available. Sugarcane is a type of tropical grass native to Asia. It was actually introduced to the New World by Christopher Columbus, who was hoping to find a favorable environment for its cultivation. I discovered that while all green plants produce sugar (sucrose) none do so as efficiently as sugarcane, which takes carbon dioxide from the air and radiation from the sun to produce sugar, which is then stored in the stalk of the plant. These stalks grow as high as fifteen feet tall and almost two inches in diameter. The first sugarcane was introduced to Florida in 1512 by Ponce de Leon. Soon this agricultural introduction was so important the area south of St. Augustine became known as "Canaveral," which meant "sugarcane field" in Spanish.

The introduction elsewhere in the Caribbean was even more successful, and by 1600, the cultivation and production of sugar had become that area's largest single industry and its second most important export, trailing only precious metals in importance to the Spanish Crown.

Commercially sugarcane is not grown from seeds, since this method of propagation does not produce a true replica of the parent. Instead, sugarcane is essentially cloned by burying stalk cuttings of preferred plant types in furrows five feet apart. In 12 months the mature cane is ready for harvest. Growers usually manage, if they've properly tended their fields, three to four harvests per year from a single planting. Each planting will continue to produce for three more years.

The harvest season for sugarcane runs between late-October and mid-March. One thing that surprised me to learn was the first step in the harvest is actually to set the cane fields on fire. This resulting inferno rids the cane of leaves and helps to prepare it for the use of mechanical harvesters.

Another surprising thing I learned was harvesting sugarcane is no longer labor-intensive. I suppose I still envisioned the sugar industry importing thousands of low-paid machete-wielding workers from the Caribbean, forcing them to work in near slave-like conditions; instead, I learned for the past twenty years, almost all sugarcane in Florida has been harvested mechanically.

Three to four harvesting machines work in tandem, accompanied by tractors which pull a veritable train of field wagons. These harvesters cut through the sugarcane at the base of the stalk, remove the tops and leaves, chop the cane into twelve-inch pieces, which are deposited in the field wagons. The cane is taken from the fields and transferred into semi-trailers, which quickly transport it to a grinding mill. Amazingly, the process is so efficient that during daylight hours, it is normal for a new nineteen-ton load of chopped cane to arrive at the mill as frequently as once every forty-five seconds.

That piece of information boggled my mind. I had to stop and think about it for a while. I suspected that one wouldn't want to be on the roads in that area during harvest time.

Reading further I learned during the season, a mill could grind as much as twenty-five thousand tons of sugarcane stalks each day. I also learned a ton of cane stalks produces two hundred pounds of raw sugar. My quick mental math showed each mill would produce five million pounds of sugar each day. I already knew there were five mills in the area, so these mills, if operating at capacity, produced over twenty-five million pounds of raw sugar every day! A season that lasts five months long. Damn! That's a lot of sugar.

I figured a lot of waste, too, but as I read on, I learned that was not the case. The mill's high-tech equipment separates the raw cane into four parts: sugar, water, molasses, and the remaining rind called bagasse. What I found to be surprising was each of these by-products is used and essentially nothing is left to waste. The water is used in the milling process. The molasses is sold off around the world as cattle feed. The bagasse actually fuels the mill's boilers, creating steam-generated electricity to power the mills. In fact, so much electricity is produced by burning bagasse that the mills' electrical output is sold to the area's electric utilities to supplement their own production. One article indicated using bagasse to power the mills eliminated the need for burning almost 115 million gallons of fossil fuel each year.

Needless to say, I was impressed. In fact, I was stunned. It seemed this industry was a far cry from being the ugly industrial polluter I had expected. I was beginning to suspect I may have been watching too much Miami Vice.

Next, I turned my attention to trying to discover who actually owns "Big Sugar." What I found was, again, surprising. I learned the industry is chiefly made up of three major players. The smallest of these entities, accounting for twenty percent of sugar production in the state, is the Peninsular Sugar Cane Growers Cooperative; a true agricultural co-op consisting of forty-five small- to medium-size member farms. The co-op grows sugarcane on approximately sixty-five thousand acres. This organization is based in the small town of Belle Glade, located on the southeastern shore of Lake Okeechobee. This entity, I quickly concluded, hardly sounded like a member of an evil sugar empire.

I read further and discovered the oldest sugar-producing organization in the state was American Sugar Corporation. This company is based in Clewiston on the south shore of the lake, a pleasant community otherwise known as "America's Sweetest Town!" American Sugar accounts for forty percent of Florida's sugar production. It was founded in 1931 by Lance Stewart, a former automobile magnate. *At last*, I thought, *finally I was on the trail of a Sugar Baron.*

I was quickly disappointed to learn much of the ownership of the firm was transferred in the 1980s to the firm's employees and today is totally owned by employees and a few charitable trusts Stewart had established. Everything I read indicated the firm was well-run and went out of its way to be open and honest both with the media and public. Heck, even the CEO was described as a scripture-quoting devout Christian.

It wasn't until I read about the last player in Florida sugar the story got more interesting. Caribbean Crystals is a privately held enterprise owned today by the Faucon family and run by two of the family's brothers, Alejandro, Jr., or Alex; and his younger brother Carlos. As a young man the patriarch of the family, Alejandro Faucon, Sr., had married into to the Gomez sugar empire in Cuba; at that time, the largest on the island.

While this family was neither particularly involved in politics, nor supportive of the Batista regime, that didn't stop the Revolution from appropriating all of the family's holdings. One story described how, following Castro's victory, a group of camouflage-clad, beret-wearing, gun-toting idealistic soldiers came to the family's mansion and quietly unfolded a map for Alejandro, Sr., and his fourteen-year-old son Alex. to see; a map that showed all of the family's properties—its fields, houses, mills, warehouses, port, everything.

The soldiers then announced: "As of this moment, this no longer belongs to you. All of it now belongs to us." Needless to say, the family quickly fled Cuba, its wealth and holdings dramatically reduced. Their destination: Palm Beach County, Florida. Their plan: to start over in the sugar industry.

Up until that time, Florida's sugar industry was tiny. That changed almost overnight. Castro's Revolution led to an embargo of Cuban-produced goods, including sugar. To help offset that shortage, the U.S. Government got involved. It quickly began to drain more of the Everglades, and provided lucrative incentives for cane producers. The Faucons were there to take advantage. As soon as they arrived, the old man purchased four thousand acres of prime cane land.

Today the family controls forty percent of Florida's sugar production, farming two hundred thousand acres of land around the eastern shore of Lake Okeechobee in western Palm Beach County, but the family didn't stop there. It is also the largest producer and exporter of sugar from the Dominican Republic, where it also owns one of the world's most luxurious and most private resorts; a place rumored to have hosted both U.S. Presidents and drug lords—reportedly at the same time!

I concluded I was on the trail of real Sugar Barons, but I knew I needed to find out more. The few details on the web hinted at political intrigue and underhanded dealings, but the information available was sketchy and incomplete. Already I was asking myself were these the people Jay Benjamin had warned about in the letter he had written to the editor? And, more importantly, were these the people who were responsible for his death? On the face of it, they seemed likely candidates, but I needed more information.

I was pondering how to get that when the phone rang.

"Hello," I answered cheerily. "This is Jim Story. How may I help you?"

"Story," a gruff voice replied. "Have you sobered up yet?"

I recognized it as belonging to none other than my friendly Sheriff's Department Investigator, Mike Collins.

"Damn, Collins, how am I supposed to answer a question like that for a member of the law enforcement community? That question sounds a lot like me being asked if I've stopped beating my wife yet."

The Lieutenant laughed and said, "That was going to be my next question." Then he continued, "You got plans for lunch today?"

I could feel a tingle run up my spine. I remembered Collins having asked that question twice before: invitations which indirectly led to me getting involved in two previous murder investigations on the island; investigations that had almost gotten me, and Jill, killed.

Chapter Fifteen

Collins and I agreed to meet for lunch at The Waterfront, a small canal-side restaurant in St. James City, famous for seafood and cold beer. I wasn't surprised that Collins had elected to come here because I knew the proprietor deeply discounted the bills of law enforcement officers. As a result, residents in town often joke that we can set our clocks by when the deputies head toward the restaurant.

The day was pleasant so we decided to dine on the back deck, a narrow wooden strip with benches and tables overlooking the canal. It's always fun to sit there since you have a good view of hungry boaters coming in to the restaurant's dock. I also enjoy reading the collection of humorous signs that decorate this space. "If you're going to drink all day, you have to start in the morning." Another proclaims, "Showers—$1; $2 If You Want to Watch." Just fun stuff like that.

The back porch also provides slightly more privacy than the main dining room, a small space that at the beginning of the twentieth century was actually St. James City's first school. We chose an empty table at the north end of the porch because of its separation from neighboring tables and because it received a little more breeze than those fully in the lee of the building. This is the kind of thing you learn to look for if you live here long.

I let Collins start the conversation, concluding he must have had a reason to ask me to lunch. He quickly got to the point.

"Jim, despite the impression I may have given, I do appreciate you letting me know about Skunkfoot's alibi. I also want to apologize in general for my recent attitude. I've been out of line, and I'm sorry about that."

I looked at him, enjoying the rare moment of having what seemed to be an upper hand with Collins. Then, after having milked the advantage for as long as possible, I replied, "Mike, I appreciate the thought, but the apology wasn't necessary. I had some of it coming."

I noticed the reappearance in his eyes of what looked more like his more normal sarcastic twinkle, and I braced myself for what was probably to come. Just as he opened his mouth to reply, he was interrupted by our waitress who wanted to know what we would be drinking. I didn't recognize her, but Mike seemed to because they exchanged a few pleasantries before she took our orders.

As she walked away I asked, "She's new here, isn't she?"

"Not really," he said. "But she hasn't worked on the island for a couple of years. I'm glad to see her back."

"Where's she been?" I innocently inquired.

Collins laughed gently. "Well, she's actually been a guest of the state. About four years ago she had taken up with a new boyfriend, a fellow new to the island. Before long he'd moved in. I guess she must have told him to make himself at home because soon he started to use a shed out back as a meth lab. I don't think she was actively involved, but then again, she didn't do anything about it either. So when we stumbled upon the operation she had a small debt to society that she needed to pay. But I'm glad to see that she's out now and working. I think she's a good person. Hopefully, she's learned her lesson."

"I guess there's more crime out here than I ever suspected," I said.

"No. There really isn't that much," Collins replied. "At least not compared to Lehigh. Usually, it's just stupid stuff, and drinking has a lot to do with that. And, of course, occasionally, you do have a few of the undereducated and unemployed who haven't yet fully comprehended that the standard of living they aspire to isn't theirs just for the taking. But for the most part, this is the quiet, safe, sleepy community you think it is. The Sheriff knows he doesn't have to assign any of his hard-assed guys out here. You may have noticed most of the deputies who work the island are pretty low key, and the instructions the Sheriff gives them are simple: Watch out for drunks and don't harass the locals."

I laughed knowing it wouldn't always be possible for the officers to honor both of those instructions. Then I decided to pull Collins's chain one more time, just to keep him honest.

"Mike, don't give me that crap. What about the SWAT team y'all sent out here a couple of months ago? There must have been at least thirty of your cars on the island, four or five ambulances, several boats, a helicopter, two armored personnel carriers, and the transporter that carried them out here. We thought we were being invaded! Was all of that really necessary?"

"It was a hostage situation," Collins replied, all traces of humor having left his face.

"Yeah, right! I heard by the time y'all got here the so-called hostage was out of the house walking down the street and the culprit was in bed sleeping off his previous night's binge."

"Okay, so we may have overreacted a little, but the perp had pulled a gun on the guy, and there were drugs involved," the Lieutenant responded grumpily.

I laughed, and replied, "I know. The way I heard it, they'd gotten drunk together down at Froggy's, and then gone home to smoke a few joints. It was all cool until the homeowner decided what he really needed was a blow job."

"Right," Mike answered, "And that's when the gun came out. According to the victim, he really wanted that blow job!"

"Apparently!" I couldn't help but laugh as I recalled the episode. "The way I heard it, the perpetrator explained as he pointed the gun at the victim, after all, it *was* his birthday!"

By this time, Mike was laughing, too. "Yeah, I guess he must have felt entitled. Anyway, the victim then walked out of the house, started wandering down the street yelling as loud as he could something about guns, drugs, and hostages. So, of course, we sent everything we had. This all went down about two o'clock in the morning, but we didn't get our full hostage team here until close to five. By that time, the birthday boy had, of course, gone soundly to sleep. But we didn't know that so we had to assume he was holed up inside, armed and dangerous. I can tell you that we had a hell of a time waking that guy up. I don't think he really came to until after the stun grenades went off."

"So," I asked. "Is he out of jail yet?"

"You know, he only spent one night with us. He lawyered up and there really wasn't that much we could charge him with. He hadn't really resisted arrest, and it was only his word against the other guy's. And it wasn't worth us pressing a misdemeanor pot charge. I guess his reputation probably took a hit, as did his bank balance, but otherwise he didn't suffer any real damage. And, besides, he and the other guy are buds again and drinking together in Froggy's almost every night."

By then our waitress had returned with our beverages and we placed our orders. He opted for a Caesar salad with broiled grouper; I requested a grouper and oyster combo basket, understanding as I did I'd likely need a nap once I returned home.

"Jim, of course, what I just said about there not being much crime out here doesn't apply when you're involved. Before you and Jill came to town, it'd been a couple of decades since there'd been a murder out here. And, from what I've been told, that crime only took about fifteen minutes to solve. But now, since y'all been here, well, it's been a little different."

"Wait a minute, Mike!" I protested. "We didn't have anything to do with causing those murders. All we did was help you find out who did."

"I know. And I do actually appreciate that. But now it seems like we've got ourselves another situation, doesn't it?"

"Did you let Frank out yet?" I asked.

"No. I've still got to verify that alibi you mentioned. In fact, I'm going to stop by Froggy's on the way out of town. It shouldn't take me more than a couple of minutes of chatting with management to find out who it was Frank left with."

"I guess then you'll have to go verify that with the lady in question?" I asked.

"I'll have to do that eventually. But I'm in no hurry. Despite what people may think, I don't really enjoy causing difficulties for people unnecessarily. And, besides, I wouldn't mind if Frank stayed with us for a while longer."

"Why's that?" I asked.

"Well, Frank being with us should help to keep the real culprit calm and give us time to quietly snoop around. And, besides, Frank's kind of entertaining. He keeps threatening to scalp one of his guards."

"So if you don't really think that Frank did it, who do you think did? Personally, I'm convinced the sugar industry was responsible for killing Jay Benjamin."

As I said that I noticed a look of amusement spread across the Lieutenant's face.

"Jim, what is it with you? Do you have something about people who have money and power? Last time, if I remember, you suggested we go after the Collier family. Now, you're thinking that Big Sugar is to blame! Trust me, Jim, those guys didn't knock Benjamin on the head."

"How can you say that? They certainly had a motive to shut him up."

"Jim, what do you really know about the sugar industry?"

I told him about the research I'd recently done and that I wanted to find out more about the industry's owners.

"Jim, you do need to know more and I can introduce you to someone to answer all your questions. Dr. Richard Duncan is a professor in the Legal Services Department out at Florida Gulf Coast University. He knows as much about Big Sugar as anyone. I guess it's just a hobby of his to know this stuff, but he knows so much about the industry the Sheriff had him come into the department a couple of years ago to give us a lecture on the subject. Would you like to meet him?"

"I'd love that."

"If he's available today, would you be willing to drive out to the campus?"

"Absolutely."

He stepped away from the table, pulled out his cell, scrolled through contacts, and dialed. A couple of minutes later he was back at the table.

"You're on at three o'clock today. That work for you?"

"You bet. Where do I meet him?"

"His office at the school." He gave me the address.

"Mike, I appreciate this a lot."

"Not a problem. I think you'll enjoy getting to know him. Give me a call tomorrow and let me know what you learn."

Chapter Sixteen

I drove my bike home, ran up the white-painted stairs of our stilt house, excitedly wanting to tell Jill about my upcoming meeting with Professor Duncan, but I'd forgotten that since I was having lunch with Lieutenant Collins, she'd decided to drive into the Cape to run a few errands (i.e., do some shopping). I wrote her a note asking her not to let me sleep past one-thirty, and then settled into my recliner. The nap was a good one, but I was able to wake up on my own, a few minutes before my self-imposed deadline. Jill wasn't back from shopping, anyway. I left her a new note that explained what I was up to and drove into Ft. Myers.

Florida Gulf Coast University is a member of the University System of Florida. Its first classes were held in 1997, but since then it has grown rapidly. Today it has almost fifteen thousand full-time students. Its campus is located near the Southwest Florida International Airport on land that had been donated by one of the state's influential founding families.

I, of course, knew about FGCU, but I'd never actually been there. I was blown away as I drove onto the campus. The buildings, of course, were all relatively new, and featured an attractive modern tropical architectural theme with green tile roofs and matching tinted windows. I was impressed.

I'd come to the school a little early just to ensure I wouldn't be late for our meeting. I had a few minutes to spare and decided to sit in the car and surf the web on my cell to learn what I could about the University. Again, I was impressed. Its multiple colleges offer more than fifty undergraduate degrees with strengths in engineering, business, hospitality services, education, health professions, nursing, rehabilitation science, and criminal justice; in short, those things important to life in twenty-first century Southwest Florida. As I further researched the criminal justice department I learned that it featured one of the nation's leading forensic sciences programs, highlighted by the largest environmental forensics facility, or 'body farm,' in the country. I hoped that Professor Duncan wouldn't feel compelled to give me a tour of that.

I knocked on his door precisely at 3 o'clock.

"Come in, Mr. Story!"

Clearly he had been expecting me. I opened the door, wondering as I did how he'd known that it was me knocking. I had been wondering what Dr. Duncan looked like. I really had no idea about how a criminal justice professor might appear. Would he resemble Dragnet's hardcore 'Just the facts, Ma'am,' ultra-uncool Jack Webb? Or would he look more like one of those modern tech guys on CSI: Miami? I would not have been surprised for him to have looked like either, but what I had certainly not expected to find was a slightly built, impressively mustachioed fellow sitting behind the desk, the spitting image, I swear, of David Suchet's depiction of Agatha Christie's legendary detective, Hercule Poirot.

The image was so striking all I could do was stare, my mouth hanging open, looking, I'm sure, like a complete idiot, but Professor Duncan must have been used to this reaction because he quickly intervened, asked me again to come inside, and invited me to take a seat in the simple chair that sat in front of his small government-issued desk.

"Dr. Duncan," I began. "I'm so sorry, but I just …I just… I just didn't expect to meet… Monsieur Poirot. Am I correct?"

"Yes, Jim," he replied warmly, his eyes lighting up at my recognition of his persona. "I appreciate that you are a fan. I'm afraid most of my students don't have a clue about who I am attempting to honor with my portrayal. And the few who can make a guess often mistake me, instead, for Inspector Clouseau."

I laughed and said, "Actually, that would have been my second guess."

He chuckled. "I would have appreciated that as well since the good Inspector is another one of my idols."

"Mine, too," I answered.

"Very good, Mr. Story, now, how may I help you?"

"Dr. Duncan, before we get started I've got to ask, how did you know that it was me at your door?"

"The little gray cells, Mr. Story!" his eyes twinkling at his little joke. "Lieutenant Collins had described for me how'd you'd likely be dressed, an old guy wearing a Columbia fishing shirt, beer can shorts, and hair in a ponytail, so I'd been watching for you when you came down the sidewalk to the building. And, then, exactly at 3 o'clock, you knocked on my door." He turned his palms up, and smiled.

"Of course," I said. "I do appreciate you taking time to meet with me, but didn't Collins explain why I was coming to see you?"

"He did briefly, saying you wanted information about the ownership of Big Sugar. But before I begin, may I ask why you're interested in this information?"

"Of course, Dr. Duncan." I explained an acquaintance had been detained for the murder of Jay Benjamin, but that I didn't believe he had done it and suspected, instead, Big Sugar may have been responsible. I went on to tell the Professor what I'd learned thus far about the production of sugar and what I was hoping to learn about the individuals that actually owned the industry. As I said this, I was pleased to note that Dr. Duncan did not laugh at me; in fact, he appeared to be taking my request seriously.

"Jim," he began, "I understand why you're asking. But, please, drop the Dr. Duncan stuff; just call me Richard."

"Got it, Richard," I answered. "An old habit I guess."

He smiled and then began, "The Sugar industry in Florida is largely owned by three entities: Peninsular Sugar Cane Growers Co-op, American Sugar Corporation, and Caribbean Crystals. The smallest, is the Peninsular Sugar Cane Growers Cooperative."

With that Richard handed me a list of the co-op's current members, organized with the largest producer at the top of the page, the smallest at the bottom. I didn't expect any of those names to mean anything to me, but I was mistaken. The name at the very top of the list was none other than The Royal Ranch! The same organization that had recently been in the news for entertaining the state's Governor and the leadership of both houses of the state's legislature at its hunting ranch in Texas. The same organization whose Florida President had recently been appointed to the Board of the Southwest Florida Water Management District, and the same organization that had recently made large, unexplained purchases of land on Pine Island. As I read this, I felt a cold sensation slide up the back of my neck.

"Richard," I exclaimed, "I thought you said the co-op was made up of small growers! Even I know the Royal Ranch is not a small player!"

He laughed. "Jim, small is a relative term, but certainly in terms of their sugar production in Florida, they are a relatively minor player. They actively grow cane on only about twelve thousand five hundred acres, although I should mention they also lease almost forty thousand acres of their land to American Sugar. Of course, the Ranch does more in the state than just grow cane. They, too, are major producers of citrus, sod, and vegetables. In fact, their citrus operation has approximately forty thousand acres of trees in the state, making them the single largest citrus producer in the U.S. So, you're right; they are not a small operation."

"Damn!" I said. "I had no idea. I thought they were primarily in Texas."

"Oh, they are," he agreed. "They own almost a million acres of land there. They are a big player in both states. Of course, Jim, I think it's important you understand the end game for them here in Florida is ultimately not just about farming. As for all the other players in sugar, it's about how, over time, to maximize the discounted cash flow values of their properties."

"What do you mean?" I asked, not sure of the distinction he was making.

"Their cash flows from growing sugar on muck land will only last a little while longer. The muck is a finite resource and it has been getting depleted for over fifty years. Some think it'll be gone in as few as five more years, so the stream of cash they've come to love is definitely going to dry up. Consequently, all of sugar is now looking for their most lucrative exit strategy."

"What do you think that'll be?" I asked.

"I think it's pretty clear. In my opinion, what the owners would like to do now, despite their protestations to the contrary, is to sell their muck to the state, hopefully at a value based upon the historical cash flows that land has generated, not at a value based upon its projected future cash flows. The difference between those two methodologies, of course, is the difference between an absolute mountain of money and a somewhat smaller but still large pile of cash."

"I can understand that," I said. "Kind of like having your cake after you've already eaten it."

The Professor laughed. "Exactly!"

"But," I asked, "What would the owners do with all that money?"

"It depends," he said. "It depends upon which group you are talking about. American Sugar, which produces almost forty percent of the sugar in the state, would like to use the money to develop their remaining area along the south shore of the lake. Their concern, not unreasonably, is to do something that would help provide long-term employment and livelihoods for all the people who have worked for them in their sugar operation, most of whom would be displaced if the state were to buy its property."

"What do you mean to develop the land? Would they try to sell it off as residential properties? And, if they did, who'd want to buy land in the Everglades?" I asked.

"Because," he answered, "It wouldn't be the Everglades by the time they'd developed it! With the right infrastructure they could sell it as prime lakefront and golf course property. The development they're envisioning would run all along the southern border of Lake Okeechobee. Keep in mind there are roughly fifty million Americans planning to retire over the next twenty years. And where do they all want to move? Florida, of course! You're familiar with what's been done at the development known as The Townships that now sprawls between Leesburg and Ocala? When they started that project no one thought anyone would want to live there either. Now, it's one of the largest, and fastest growing, cities in the whole country."

"But," I objected, "Development like that along the lake would be an ecological disaster. If that happened, there would be no way to ever redirect the flow of water from the lake back into the Glades! Once people start to live there you could never make that happen."

"You're right, of course," Dr. Duncan said. "But I suspect that is not exactly the top priority for the owners of all that land. I'd point out this group has already filed a request with the regional Water Management Board for authorization to develop a whole new city in the area, a community with ten thousand new single family homes."

I stared at him, shocked by what I had just heard. Then I asked, "You said this is what American Sugar would like to do. What about what the other players?"

"I don't know what all the members of the co-op have in mind, but I do know the Royal Ranch would like to buy up and develop Pine Island with what it gets out of the deal. Jim, since you live on Pine Island perhaps you've heard about this already?"

"We've heard they are buying up property, but no one knows what they're planning to do on the island. But I hear you saying they're not planning to grow mangoes and palm trees."

The Professor laughed and said, "No. I'm afraid not."

"Dr. Duncan—" I stopped and began again. "I'm sorry, Richard, what about Caribbean Crystals? What do they want to do? Benjamin's letter said something about someone wanting the casino gambling rights for Dade and Broward counties."

"Jim, they most certainly want that, but the Faucons, the family who owns Caribbean Crystals, thinks about a much bigger picture than that. You have, of course, recently read about President Obama's steps to normalize our country's relationship with Cuba?"

"Of course," I answered, wondering as I did how this could possibly relate to the Florida sugar industry.

"If you cut to the chase," the Professor said, "He took this step because the Faucons wanted him to because, if you will, the Faucons want to once again own Cuba."

I could see him studying my face for reaction, noting I'm sure a look of complete skepticism.

"Mr. Story, I know this is hard to believe, but please let me explain. The Faucon family was at one time the largest sugar producer in Cuba until it was driven out when Castro's revolution seized all of their properties. But now the Castros are both near death, and their socialist revolution, which, of course, was always doomed to be an utter failure, has left the people of the island destitute. For many years the country was supported by the Russians, but they had to cut it loose. Then Venezuela's Chavez funneled some of that country's oil wealth to support the island in order to irritate the U.S., but now that's dried up, too. China's always been too intelligent and too strategic to waste good money there. Putin would like to do something there again, just to ridicule Obama, but with falling oil prices there's only so much he can do. So now the whole place is crumbling and the rats are starting to jump ship. Essentially, the whole country is up for sale or will be as soon as Fidel kicks the bucket. The Spanish, the Brazilians, and the Canadians have a big head start on us since they've been doing business there for decades while we've been twiddling our thumbs, restricted by the silly trade embargo we've enforced for domestic political reasons. The Faucons, of course, could see what was happening. And they didn't like it since it has always been the family's dream to return to their homeland. Alejandro, Jr. has been going back to the island since 2012. There's a famous photo taken then of him standing in front of the family's former mansion in Havana, his boyhood home, with tears in his eyes. Whether he was crying because he was overcome by finally being home or because he was just ticked off that others had gotten a head start on his plans to cheaply buy up the choicest parts of the island, it's hard to say. But, finally, the family felt that it couldn't afford to wait any longer, and once Obama and the Democrats got their butts kicked in the last election, they demanded the U.S. get back into Cuba ASAP."

"You've got to be kidding me!" I said. "There's no way that anyone could make things happen like that."

"Jim, trust me on this. To further illustrate, let me back up to your question about who owns the sugar industry. In the interest of time I'm going to keep the story to the basics. One of those players, as you already know, is American Sugar, a closely held corporation owned jointly by its employees and a few charitable trusts. This group is based in Clewiston, rather, I should say, this group is Clewiston. It's as solid a group as you'll find anywhere in the state. And, politically, one of the most influential. The only group politically stronger is the other major sugar player, Caribbean Crystals, and its owner, the Faucon family. I know you already know the history of this family, so I won't bore you with that information. Instead, let me just cut to the chase. The reason I know they didn't kill Jay Benjamin is they don't have to do something like that to get what they want. You, of course, know the name Monica Lewinsky?"

I looked at Dr. Duncan like he'd suddenly become the Absent Minded Professor. What could President Clinton's promiscuous, blue dress-wearing, love-struck intern possibly have to do with sugar and with whomever had killed Jay Benjamin? Had he lost track of why we were meeting?

"Of course!" I protested. "What does she have to do with any of this?"

The Professor calmly continued, "I bring up her name simply to illustrate how powerful the Faucon family is. On President's Day, 1996, Bill Clinton and Monica Lewinsky were secluded in the Oval Office. On this occasion, Clinton was telling her that he no longer felt right about their relationship and they had to put a stop to it. But, according to Lewinsky, this was the very moment when, despite the normal arrangement in place during their meetings, a phone call was put through to the President. This call was from none other than Alex Faucon. They spoke, according to White House records, for twenty-two minutes. But, according to Lewinsky's testimony, the conversation was one-sided, with Faucon spending most of that time loudly yelling at Clinton. It was later determined Faucon had called the President to complain that, a few hours before, Vice President Gore had called for legislation to levy a penny-a-pound tax on Florida sugar growers to help restore the Everglades. I tell you this story to give you an idea about the kind of political power this family has. If they can interrupt the President of the United States at a time like that, and then scream at him, then they can pretty much do what they want to do. By the way, that tax was never passed."

"But that was a long time ago."

"Trust me, their influence has not diminished. It has gotten stronger. Let me tell you about the family's alignment with the two political parties. The family's older brother, Alejandro, Jr., or Alex, has always been a Democrat, but when Bush and Clinton were running for the Presidency it was far from clear which of them would win. So being the pragmatists they are, the family decided that the younger brother, Carlos, would have to become a Republican, becoming overnight one of the largest donors to that Party, at both state and national levels. So now they were among the largest donors to both parties, controlling some would say, their most important political players at all levels. As an example, it is known annually the family makes significant contributions to nearly fifty members of the U.S. House Committee on Agricultural. In the past decade, it has been estimated they have donated almost twenty million dollars to politicians in Washington and multiples of that amount in Florida. It is not a stretch to say there is not an important politician in either Tallahassee or Washington who isn't on a first name basis with one brother, or the other, or both. Our current Governor, for example, received much of his reelection funds from the Faucon family. And the largest political contributions to both of our state's current U.S. Senators, one a Democrat, one a Republican, come from one Faucon or the other. And who, you might ask, are among the largest contributors to the Presidential exploration efforts of Hillary Clinton, Jeb Bush, and Marco Rubio? But their influence isn't limited to Tallahassee and Washington. Most of the county commissioners in all of South Florida's counties, for example, rely on this family for large portions of their campaign dollars. I could go on, but I think I've made my point. When you 'own' Presidents, you don't need to go around killing small-time ex-politicians who are trying to make nuisances of themselves. Benjamin, as I'm sure you already know, had already been forced out of his county commission seat by a candidate whose campaign was largely funded by sugar's owners. And you can trust me, if that wasn't enough to rid them of his interference, they would have had other means at their disposal."

"What do you mean?" I asked.

"I'll simply say that sugar wasn't the only white crystalline substance important to our dearly beloved late County Commissioner."

"What?! You mean cocaine?"

"I'll let you ask Lieutenant Collins about that. I'm sure he knows more about that subject than I do. Now, Jim, I'm going to have to excuse myself. I have a roomful of impatient graduate students waiting on me to entertain and elucidate."

"Certainly," I stammered. "And thank you so much for all of this information."

As I walked back to my car my head was spinning. Could I believe what this dandified professor had just told me? Were the sugar people really so powerful they wouldn't worry about Jay Benjamin and what potential future revelations he might make? And what was really going on with the Royal Ranch and its recent purchases on Pine Island? Was Big Sugar involved in this too? What had Duncan meant when he had said the ex-commissioner had something to do with cocaine? Was he a user? A dealer? A smuggler? And did any of this relate, somehow, someway, to President Obama's newly announced Cuba policy? Was Big Sugar behind this also? Did the Faucons really have that much power? Bottom line—if Professor Duncan was correct that Big Sugar wouldn't have killed Jay Benjamin, then who had? I knew there was a long list of others with possible motivations to have done him in. Truthfully, I had to admit to myself I didn't have a clue. All I could do was shake my head and be thankful solving this crime was Lieutenant Collins' responsibility, not mine.

Chapter Seventeen

I called Jill as soon as I was on the road. I started telling her all of what I had heard from the Professor, but quickly stopped, understanding I couldn't really do it justice over the phone. I also feared as unbelievable as the information was, if I didn't tell her in person, she'd probably conclude I'd spent the afternoon at Woody's, or Froggy's, or Ragged Ass, or Bert's, or one of the other bars on the island. So I told her I'd explain as soon as I got home. Unfortunately, it took me a lot longer to get there than I'd anticipated.

By the time I'd left the University, Ft. Myers' traffic was in rush hour mode, bumper to bumper and moving slowly. Living on the island, I'd forgotten how frustrating that can be. Unfortunately, the closer I got to the bridge over the river, the worse the traffic was. Eventually, I tuned in a local radio station to get a traffic report and learned there had been an accident on the Mid-Point Bridge, the one I planned to use. The Caloosahatchee River runs between Ft. Myers and Cape Coral, and I had to cross the river to get back to Pine Island. There are other bridges, of course, but by this time they, too, would be backing up. I really had no good choices. I could stay where I was and hope the accident cleared soon or I could attempt to work my way across town to get onto one of the other bridges. In the end, I decided to just stay where I was. Fortunately, the bridge cleared in about forty-five minutes. I calculated with that delay I should be able to get home by six, but that calculation didn't consider that the new draw bridge in Matlacha was stuck, as it often is, in the open position. Consequently, traffic trying to get onto the island was backed up all the way onto Veterans' Parkway. My blood pressure, no longer used to the stress of living off-island, felt like it was probably heading into the danger zone, but at least these delays gave me time to think.

After mulling over what Dr. Duncan had told me, I decided his conclusion that the Faucons would not need to resort to violence against Jay Benjamin, despite me wishing otherwise, probably made sense. I also concluded I still didn't have a dog in this fight; I really didn't need to be concerned about who had killed Benjamin, at least, I wouldn't as soon as Collins verified Frank's alibi and let him out of jail, but for the life of me, I couldn't much get beyond these points. Someone had knocked Benjamin in the head, apparently with Frank's shark club, and someone had stuffed his body in one of Frank's dumpsters on North Captiva Island. Those were the facts. Frank had threatened Benjamin with a Seminole Curse. Benjamin had been having an affair with the wife of someone on the island. But so, too, apparently, had Frank. That led me to scratch my head over whom Frank's lady friend might have been because it was actually hard to believe any lady on the island would have been that desperate for affection. Then again, it has been my experience the reasons underlying the romantic taste of women are not always obvious. My mind had just started to drift into mulling over my experience with those kinds of female mysteries when traffic began to move. I gave Jill a call to update her. Since my ETA was now somewhat after seven, we decided to just meet for dinner at one of our favorite island restaurants.

Red's is one of the island's nicer dining establishments and one of the few places where you can order something other than the usual fried fish or sandwich options. It also has a great bar. Consequently, it isn't unusual for us to find our neighbors and friends clustered there, but as I drove into the parking lot I didn't recognize any of their cars. I did notice, however, Jill had beaten me to the restaurant and had already gone inside, probably to stake out our favorite stools at the bar.

Because the lot was nearly full, I had to park toward the rear. Not a big deal, but as I was walking through the lot toward the door I had to step out of the way of a large, dirty, noisy new-model diesel pickup. It looked like a Ford F-250, probably someone's work truck. As the truck drove by, I was able to make out a name tastefully stenciled on the driver's door: The Royal Ranch. Damn. Was this a coincidence? I told myself to pay attention to the truck's occupants when they came into the restaurant. As it turned out, I really didn't have to make that much of an effort.

I found Jill sitting as I had expected; in the middle of the bar strategically positioned in front of the small television. She was engaged, as is her norm, in conversation with the ladies whom tend the bar, Amy and Andy. Both as nice as can be but professional and experienced practitioners of their trades, easily able to engage in conversation with anyone. I think, however, they probably actually enjoyed talking with Jill, because as I arrived, they were sharing iPhone photos of their grandchildren. I could hear them emitting "oohs" and "aahs" as I settled onto the stool next to Jill, moving her purse out of the way as I did. Eventually, they recognized me, put their phones away, and Andy moved toward the bar to prepare my customary Johnny Walker Red and water in a tall glass.

As we began to chat, and as my drink arrived, I noticed the occupants of the Royal Ranch pickup slide into the two stools immediately to my right. I moved my stool slightly to the left, trying to ensure they had plenty of room, having noticed the truck's driver was on the large side; I guessed six-foot-six and weighing close to three hundred pounds. He noticed my effort to accommodate him, thanked me, but told me not to worry; he had plenty of room. As they settled in, Amy moved over to take their drink orders.

I gave Jill a quick kiss to say hello. She asked me immediately how my conversation with Dr. Duncan had gone. I told her it had been great, but immediately tried to redirect the conversation, asking instead, how her day had been. She gave me a questioning look, confused about my motives, but before she could ask, I turned toward her, putting a finger to my lips, and pointing discreetly in the direction of the fellows sitting on my right. She caught on and quickly transitioned into a dialogue about the lovely blouses she'd bought at Belk's. I listened intently, but once she came to a stop, I gave her a wink and turned toward the guys on my right.

I held out my hand in a friendly manner, offered a handshake, and introduced myself. "Hello. My name is Jim."

The big guy accepted the offer, grasped my extended hand in his significantly larger and calloused paw, and gave it a powerful squeeze.

"Good to meet you, Jim. My name is Hector but my friends call me Bull. This fellow here," indicating the scrawny, shaggy-haired, rangy fellow sitting on his right, "is Bubba."

"Nice to meet y'all. This is my wife, Jill."

"Glad to meet you, ma'am. It's always a pleasure to be introduced to a beautiful lady," Bull replied.

I was thinking to myself, after he added that last part, about the possible origin of his nickname, but I decided not to pursue that question at this time. Instead, I got right to the reason for me wanting to talk with them.

"Bull, I couldn't help but notice as y'all drove in it looks like y'all work for the Royal Ranch?"

"That we do, Jim. We moved here about a month ago to take care of some of the Ranch's property out here."

"Yeah, I read in the paper your company bought some palm farms here on Pine Island. So y'all live here full-time?"

"I guess you could say that. Right now we're staying in one of the company's trailers up in Bokeelia."

"That's cool. What, if you don't mind me asking, are y'all doing with the property? Clearing it?"

"No, not really. We're kind of just cleaning it up some and watching out for the place. We've got a tractor, a mower, and some other stuff to knock down the weeds and keep it neat, but we're primarily there just to take care of the trees and make sure there's nobody squatting on the property, growing pot on it, or any other stupid stuff."

"Bull, that doesn't sound like a way for the Ranch to make much money. What's the long-term plan for the property?"

"Now, Jim, that kind of question's above my pay grade. I just do what my boss tells me to do."

I thought I could sense from his reply Bull was starting to get a little nervous about my curiosity, but before I lost him totally I hoped to ask another question or two.

"Bull, I don't know if you are aware of this, but a lot of folks out here are curious about what the Royal Ranch is planning to do on the island. You know, a lot of them don't want to see anything out here change, and they are worried y'all aren't out here just to grow palm trees. Personally, I don't care that much, but there are a lot of tree huggers out here that do. In fact, one of them, a guy named Jay Benjamin, just went and got himself killed. Y'all hear about that?"

"Jim, you ain't suggesting that we did that guy, are you?"

"Oh, no! Of course not," I quickly answered. "I didn't mean to imply that. It's just that we're all getting scared about what's going on. None of us know what to think anymore."

"Yeah, I can understand that. But, look, Jim, we didn't have anything to do with that. Me and Bubba are good people, and I can tell you the people we work for are good folks, too. Now, if y'all will excuse us, I think our table's ready. Amy, my dear, could you please move our tab to our table? Nice to meet you, ma'am."

With that they both stood up and moved back towards the hostess's stand. I guessed their table wasn't really ready, but Bull had probably grown tired of being accused of murder. I didn't blame him. I thought he'd handled the accusation better than I would have.

Jill apparently thought so, too. "Jim, that wasn't very nice. Why on earth would you think those nice guys killed Jay Benjamin? And let me remind you that you are not responsible for finding out who did."

"Yeah. You're right. But let me tell you what I learned today at the University." I proceeded to tell her everything Dr. Duncan had told me, emphasizing, of course, what I had learned about the Royal Ranch's involvement with the sugar industry and ending with the Professor's summary that people who owned presidents didn't need to kill people who annoyed them.

I could see Jill mulling over that information. Eventually she replied, "That makes sense to me. Now, let's order something to eat."

As we waited on our food I noticed Bull and Bubba had been seated in a booth near the door, a spot we'd have to pass on our way out.

"Jill, let me ask you a question. Who do you think Frank is having an affair with?"

She laughed. "Jim, I really think Kenny must be confused. For the life of me I can't imagine any of our friends doing anything like that with him."

"But that's what he said. And that's what I told Mike Collins. He was going to try to talk with Jenna down at Froggy's to see if she knew who he might have been with. But I don't know if he ever did. I'm going to try to talk with him tomorrow, and if I do, I'll try to find out what he learned."

"Jim, I'm telling you right now none of my girlfriends are having an affair with Frank Osceola."

"Well, if that's true, that's bad for Frank. Without an alibi for the night Benjamin was killed, Frank is likely to be convicted of his murder."

"Frank didn't kill him, Jim."

"Who did, Jill?"

"Damn, Jim. Who do you think I am, Miss Marple?"

"No, but I did meet Hercule Poirot today!" I laughed and told her about how the Professor had looked during our meeting today.

"Well, Jim maybe we need to start using our own little gray cells. Let's start by eliminating as many suspects as we can, and see who we have left."

"I'm with you. Who can we eliminate?"

"Jim, we can start with Frank. I'm willing to bet on that, alibi or not."

"Okay with me. What do you think about Big Sugar?"

"We should eliminate them, too. I think the Professor's right about that."

"How about the Royal Ranch? Do you think Bull and Bubba could have done it? They are on the island and Benjamin might have been unhappy about their company's investment out here."

"Jim, my gut is telling me they are okay. Bull told us they were good people. He could have reacted a lot differently, but there was just something about how he told us they were good people that sounded convincing to me. I know that's not a lot, but I'm willing to go with that for now. So if we cross off all of these suspects, who do we have left?"

"Well, we've got the husband of your friend in the Hookers whom Benjamin was seen with at the Seminole Casino Hotel. And there are some developers and realtors on the island who hated him. Of course, we can't rule out the Seminole Curse."

"Yeah, and don't forget about what Duncan told me about cocaine. Anytime drugs are involved there's always a possible motive."

"So, big guy, what do you suggest we do next?"

"I'm going to talk with Mike and see what he can tell me about the cocaine tie in. You need to talk with your girlfriends and try to learn which one of them was sleeping with Skunkfoot."

"That didn't happen, trust me."

"We'll see. You ready to go?"

"Yeah. But let me get a 'to go' box from Andy."

Then with Jill's fried calamari safely secured, we headed toward the door, waving to Bull and Bubba on our way out.

Chapter Eighteen

The next morning I called Lieutenant Collins.

"Mike, this is Jim Story. Are you available for lunch today?"

"I can be. Where you want to meet?"

"How about Little Lilly's Deli? It's Thursday and that means chili. Have you ever had Matt's chili?"

"Oh, yeah! It's the best on the island. See you at twelve."

Little Lily's Island Deli is one of our island's most delicious secrets. It's a small breakfast and lunch spot, almost hidden in a back nook of an inconspicuous island-style shopping complex. It's the kind of place if you don't know it's there, you won't just stumble across it, which is fine with me. It's much too nice of a place to be overrun by tourists. And too small. For lunch it features a fine array of handmade sandwiches that you can have customized any way you wish, unique salads, and each day there's a different homemade soup. It's the kind of place where you order at the counter, go find a seat either in the adjoining room or at a table on the deck in front of the building, and wait for a staff member to deliver your food. It's also the kind of place that is fun, deriving its vibe from the attitude of the deli's matriarch and owner. There's whimsical island artwork on the walls, unique sets of artsy salt and pepper shakers on each table, a restroom decorated like a disco, and the staff, well, their piercings and hair colors frequently change, seemingly to match their usually pleasant moods. It's a very popular place for islanders to eat.

Collins and I both ordered the daily special, upsizing our sandwiches to whole-sized despite anticipating the accompanying cup of chili, which really is great. Because the weather was pleasant we elected to sit at a table on the deck. He chose a chair that put his back to the restaurant, leaving me to sit exposed to the parking lot. I understood this was likely a necessary professional habit on his part.

"So, Jim, how'd your conversation with Dr. Duncan go?"

"Actually, Mike, I thought it went rather well. I enjoyed meeting him. He's a neat guy and I learned a lot of interesting information."

"Good. So I gather you must not have accused him of looking like Inspector Clouseau?"

"No, fortunately I guessed correctly, but we did discuss Clouseau briefly. And, I must say I couldn't help but think of you then given your resemblance to Inspector Dreyfus!"

"Damnit, Jim. Just when I thought we were getting back to being on good terms you have to go and say something like that. But you did get the information you were looking for?"

"Yeah. I think so and more. Bottom line, he convinced me Big Sugar wouldn't need to kill Benjamin."

"Do you buy that, Jim?"

"I think so. Do you?"

"Always have."

"He did say, however, I should ask you about Benjamin and cocaine."

The Lieutenant instantly became stone-faced. Then he said, "Jim, you do know, don't you, that you can't believe *everything* that little dandified dude tells you?"

"Mike, don't give me that crap. You're the one who sent me out there to talk to the guy. You obviously believe he knows what he's talking about. And he told me to ask you. So what's it about?"

"Jim, what I'm going to tell you goes no further than this table. This is not public information and you are not hearing it from me. The Sheriff in Lee County, as you know, is an elected official. And our current Sheriff, my boss, is as popular a politician as there is in the county. But the Sheriff Department's budget has to be approved each year by the County Commission. Consequently, the relationships between the Sheriff and each of the Commissioners is, to say the least, somewhat unusual. It's been my observation my boss tries to go out of his way not to embarrass any of them. A few years ago, for example, we learned that a commissioner had become deeply involved in the drug scene, and along with that, was into some other pretty kinky stuff. We could have easily busted the guy on a couple of occasions, but the Sheriff tried privately to warn the guy, told him what we knew, and advised him to clean up his act. In that case, the Commissioner elected, instead, to resign. A few weeks after he was out of office we did end up arresting him for trying to buy heroin while in the company of a known transvestite prostitute. But he'd had his chance. The same kind of chance we gave Benjamin."

"What do you mean?"

"Our beloved late Commissioner was many things, Jim. He was a very popular politician, serving in office for over twenty years. He was an extremely effective public communicator, and he was one of the area's most passionate advocates for the environment. But there were also aspects of his personality that were not as positive. For example, he was, shall we say, a 'hound dog' of the highest order. He would not, apparently *could* not, leave the fairer sex alone. And they loved him, too. I guess it was his mix of charm, power, sensitivity, good looks, and compassion that tended to make him irresistible to certain types of women. He cut, shall we say, a particularly wide swath through the ladies in leadership positions of many of the area's environmental organizations. But, unfortunately, his appetites weren't just limited to simple lust. He had to take things further than that. There was something in his makeup that made him want to take his conquests to places they had never been before; he had to make them do things they would otherwise never have done. Apparently, that was what really turned him on; what really made him feel like a man. And one of the ways he did that was, over time, to introduce his seductees to the pleasures of old-fashioned cocaine snorting. Eventually, of course, we got wind of what he was doing and the Sheriff warned him off. And I guess he stopped or at least he became more careful. We didn't hear any more about that kind of stuff, even once he was out of office, so I guess he must have gone clean. But, as you know, he still couldn't leave the women alone, and they him."

"What did Duncan mean when he said Big Sugar wouldn't have needed to kill Benjamin since they knew about his cocaine issues?"

"I'm sure they'd collected enough pictures over the years to have been able to completely discredit him should that have ever become necessary."

"Yeah. That makes sense."

As we were concluding this conversation, Collins noticed a car pull up in the parking lot and watched the occupant, a sturdily built bearded fellow wearing well-made twill trousers, the cuffs of which were stuffed inside the tops of a pair of khaki hiking boots. It was obvious that Collins and this fellow recognized each other because, as the new arrival climbed the stairs to the deck, they waved. Then I, too, recognized him. It was Bill McClelland, the retired lawyer, environmental activist, and island expert I had last seen at the recent meeting of the Pine Island Improvement Association, the meeting at which Jay Benjamin had spoken. He, of course, didn't have the foggiest idea who I was, but I was delighted when he turned to walk over to speak with us. Collins shook his hand and then introduced me. We shook hands, too.

"Mike, it's good to see you. I've been hoping I might run into you, just to see how you're doing on determining who killed Jay Benjamin. You know Jay was one of my best friends, and a guy I thought the absolute world of. I want to see the bastard who killed him put away forever."

"Bill, trust me, we all do."

"So are you making any progress?"

"We're holding a person of interest, but we're still in the process of gathering evidence. We've got a long ways to go."

"Was it that silly barge jockey? That's the word on the island."

"Bill, sorry, but I'm not at liberty to discuss the particulars of the case."

I could tell that Mike wanted to change the subject because he then asked McClelland, "Did you come down here to get some of Matt's chili?"

"You bet. It's the best. But I'm really here to meet Amanda Johnson. We want to talk about the new shrimp farm. Y'all haven't seen her, have you?"

"Nope."

"Well, I guess I'll wait for her inside. It was good meeting you, Jim; and, Mike, if there's anything I can do to help your investigation, let me know. If that crazy renegade killed Jay, I want to see him get what's coming to him."

"Good seeing you, Bill," the Lieutenant replied.

After he left, I said to Mike, "He said he was meeting Amanda Johnson. That's the lady whom Jill told me was seen having a real good time with Benjamin over at the Seminole Hard Rock on the east coast. Did y'all look into that?"

"Yeah. We did. It didn't take us asking many questions to identify her, but that didn't really lead anywhere. She and her husband had gone up north together to attend the wedding of a family member when the murder took place. We eliminated them early on."

"Speaking of marital infidelity, y'all still have Frank locked up?"

"Sure do. He still refuses to tell us what he was doing on the night in question. He can't provide an alibi, and, until he does, he's going to continue to be our guest."

"Were you able to find out from the folks at Froggy's who the supposed lady in question was?"

"Yeah. That wasn't hard either and we've spoken with her. She admits she and Frank might have been together on the night in question, but that's all she'll give us. So until we've got more than that, Frank stays where he is."

"Do I know her?"

"Don't know if you do or not, Jim."

"You're not going to tell me who she is, are you?"

"Nope. How's your chili?"

Chapter Nineteen

"Hey, Jim! What's up?"

"Kenny, I need to ask you a question."

"Uh, oh. I can tell you right now, I didn't do it!"

"Oh, shut up, Kenny. This is serious. You told me the other day Frank couldn't have killed Jay Benjamin because he was with a woman the night it went down. Were you sure about that?"

"Absolutely."

"When you say they were together do you mean like they were together as in sleeping together?"

"Well, that's what I assumed. After all, they did leave Froggy's arm in arm about ten o'clock at night. And they damn sure acted like they wanted to keep it a secret. Why else would they have done that?"

"What do you mean about not talking about it? What'd they do, make you swear an oath or something?"

"Exactly."

"But you told me?"

"No, Jim, I didn't. I told you Frank couldn't have murdered Benjamin because he was with a woman, but I didn't tell you who the woman was. And I won't."

"Do I know her?"

"Yep. You know her and her husband—well."

"Are they full-timers?"

"Nope."

"Own their home here?"

"Yep."

"Friends?"

"Yep."

"You won't tell me who she is?"

"Jim, I can't. But I did over hear her say that they were going to spend the night together, and they were both pretty giggly about it."

"Giggly?"

"You know, laughing and carrying on like they were having fun, but they were about to go do something that they shouldn't."

"And she was there without her husband?"

"Yep. She walked in by herself, went up to Frank, gave him a quick kiss on the cheek, and then they left. And all of this took place, I believe, while her husband was down at Woody's playing Open Mic Night."

I looked at Kenny like he'd lost his mind. In his own way, he'd just let me know who the couple in question was, but I knew there was absolutely no way this couple could be having marital issues. If there were ever a couple deeply in-love, it was them. And I knew they'd been that way since they'd gone to the same grade school back in Ohio. They did everything together, and when you saw them, you could almost see the affection they had for each other. Their love simply dripped off of them. This made no sense.

"Kenny, you haven't started smoking dope, have you? There is no way that Lillian would ever be having an affair with Frank."

"Whoa, Jim. I never mentioned Lillian's name, did I?"

"No, you didn't, but I don't know anyone in town other than her husband who would have been playing Open Mic Night. Am I wrong?"

"Jim, you can guess all you want to, and you're pretty good with your guessing, but I can't tell you who the lady in question was."

"Got it. Thanks."

"Jill!"

I couldn't wait to tell her what I'd just learned from Kenny.

"Jill!! Where are you?"

I finally found her by the canal, staring at the dock's bare, untreated wood.

"Jill, you're not going to believe what—"

"Jim, this dock is a mess. We need to get this finished."

"I'm going to get to it. The hard part is done. I just haven't had time. There's a lot going on, you know?"

"Jim, no offense, but I think we need to have someone come finish this. It's really looking bad, and there's no telling how long it's going to take before you have enough time to finish it."

"Jill, I'll get to it, but this thing with Frank has distracted me."

"Honey, no offense, but I've seen you like this before. You've got enough to worry about, and there's no telling how long it's going to take you to get back to this. Why don't you just call

Johnny and see how much he'd charge to put a couple of coats of stain on it? It shouldn't be that much."

"But—"

"Jim, please, I think you ought to call him."

"OK. But I'm not going to pay him too much money."

"Jim…"

"Jill, wait until you hear what I've got to tell you. This is really something."

I proceeded to explain I'd learned from Kenny who Frank had been with the night of the murder.

"Jim, why don't you go ahead and call the asylum, too, and ask if they've got a vacancy. You have to be crazy if you think Lillian would ever be having an affair with Frank Osceola. I mean I love Frank, and this is not a reflection on him, but she and her husband are just so much in-love. They've been sweethearts since they were kids and you can tell they still love each other very much. I think you and Kenny are both nuts!"

"Jill, I agree with you. I didn't say I thought they were having an affair; I just said they were together the night in question, but for some reason, neither of them will talk about it. I wonder why that is?"

"Hummmm. That's interesting. I'm going to see her in a couple of night at Hookers'. I'll make you a deal. I'll talk to her and see what she'll tell me, but you've got to call Johnny."

"You've got a deal."

We went inside. Jill wandered downstairs to resume her work putting together the 'silent auction basket' that she was planning to donate for the Hookers' upcoming wine tasting event. The Matlacha

Hookers is an island-based civic organization that does wonderful work on the island, raising annually from a host of different events almost fifty thousand dollars for donation to charitable and educational groups on the island. And they have fun doing it.

The annual wine tasting, which is open to the public, is always one of the year's most enjoyable events. Various local businesses donate wine to be auctioned, and between that, the members' silent auction baskets, and concessions, the group usually manages to clear five thousand dollars from the event. I am delighted Jill is active in this group. It does good work.

I decided I might as well go ahead, bite the bullet, and call Johnny about finishing the dock.

Johnny is one of the island's real characters. He's lived there all of his life and looks the part. His most noticeable feature is a healthy gray beard that drops almost to his navel. He usually gets around town on a bicycle, and I've noticed if he's riding into the wind that beard will blow back over his shoulder. In the past he's made a living as a fisherman, a crabber, and by working construction, but now that the construction boom is over he gets by doing odd jobs. He's good at what he does.

"Johnny, this is Jim Story. I was hoping that I could talk with you again about staining my dock."

"Jim, good to hear from you. How's my favorite lady, Miss Jill, doing?"

"She's fine, Johnny. Thanks for asking. But about my dock—"

"Jim, I heard down at the Tiki you had already tackled that project by yourself. Did that turn out okay for you?"

"Well, Johnny, as a matter of fact, I haven't quite finished it yet, and that's—"

"I sure hope you didn't screw it up, Jim. You know if you don't strip off the old stain properly you can end up with a real mess on your hands. If you did that it could end up costing a lot more than the quote I gave you the first time."

"Johnny, I haven't screwed up the damn dock. I just did all the hard work for you. I've already pressure washed it. All it needs now is to have someone put brightener and stain on it. Probably shouldn't take you more than a day. I'd finish it, but I don't have time right now, so I thought I'd see if you'd be interested in doing it for me. I'm willing to pay you a couple of hundred dollars. I already have the supplies."

"Jim, there's one thing I really hate, and that's having to come in and fix something after an amateur has screwed it up trying to do it himself because he's too cheap to pay me to do it right the first time. Normally, I'd tell you or anyone else in this situation to go take a hike. But, truth is, Jim, I need to talk to you about something. How about if I come over the day after next to take a look at the dock again? We can talk about the price then."

"That sounds good. About nine in the morning?"

"I'll see you then."

I was a little steamed about Johnny having concluded I'd probably screwed up the dock, but at the same time, I was glad he said he would come over. Truthfully, I was starting to be more interested in getting Frank out of jail and finding out who killed Benjamin than I was in restaining my dock. Besides, now I was curious what Johnny wanted to talk to me about.

Chapter Twenty

Early the next day Jill and I were in the midst of our morning ritual—tea, scrolling through electronic devices, reading the morning's newspaper—when I asked about her plans for the day.

"I'm thinking I'll go into to the Cape this morning. I need to find some stuff for the baskets. How about you? You want to ride with me?"

"Oh, hell, no! Not if you're going to a craft store. You know I get the heebie jeebies anytime I go near one of those places."

"Yes. I remember. So, if not that, what are you going to do?"

"It's a nice day. Sun's shining. Not much wind. I'm thinking about going out on the Sound and riding up to North Captiva for lunch."

"North Capitva, huh? Going to have a look at where Jay Benjamin was killed?"

I gave her my best innocent and surprised look. "Oh, I'd totally forgotten that's where they found his body, but that's not why I was going. I just thought it'd be a nice day to ride up and have lunch at Barnacle's. Maybe see Jamie. She's still working there, isn't she?"

"As far as I know. Look, Jim, that sounds like a nice way to spend the day, but please try to stay out of trouble."

"Of course! I'm just going up to have lunch. How much trouble could I get in?"

She gave me her look, the one where she rolls her eyes to convey a sense of exasperation, a look I knew well. With that she disappeared upstairs. I went in the opposite direction and quickly gathered rods and reels, a cooler stocked with water and ice, my tackle bag, and the keys to the boat. Five minutes later the boat was in the water. I fired it up, blew the horn to alert Jill I was leaving, and motored toward the Sound.

I love getting on the water this time of year, especially during the middle of the week when there's usually little boating traffic. On a day like today you normally don't have to stress about getting run over or being bounced around by the wakes of passing boats. Even the fish and birds seem to enjoy the relative peace and quiet. As soon as I exited the canal they were putting on a show. Pelicans were dive-bombing bait schools; schools noisily stirring the water's surface. Every time I see this occurring, I conclude being a bait fish would probably not be a good thing. Not only are you threatened from above, but you are also constantly harassed from underneath by foraging trout, red fish, snook, or other predators. I watched the show for a minute, and then noticed closer to the mangroves, mullet leaping before flopping, seemingly happily, back to their liquid habitat. They, too, were probably being harassed. Nobody knows for sure why mullet jump. I prefer to believe they leap just for the fun of it. I certainly hope so.

Minutes later the boat was on an easy plane as I began the run toward North Captiva. This island is the third in the line of barrier islands that separates Pine Island Sound from the Gulf of Mexico. To the south lay Sanibel and Captiva; to the north, Cayo Costa. Until 1921, North Captiva was actually part of what was then a much larger Captiva Island. But on that date a fierce hurricane cut through the island and formed what is now known as Redfish Pass.

There are no bridges that connect to North Captiva. Consequently, for many years the island was largely deserted, but eventually the appeal of living on a deserted island proved too strong, development began, and by the turn of the century, hundreds of expensive vacation homes had been constructed on the northern end of the island. But Hurricane Charley struck the island in 2004, destroyed one hundred sixty homes, and severely damaged even more. Reconstruction from that storm continues today, but even the damage from Charley has not been enough to persuade folks from wanting to build on what is not much more than a sand bar. New construction is booming; construction that keeps Frank Osceola's barge profitably engaged, and the dumpster in which Jay Benjamin's body was found full.

While the northern end of the island has been developed, to the south much of the island is owned by the State of Florida; at least what is left of that portion of the island. When Charley came ashore it severed the island and washed away five hundred yards of pristine beach. For many months, it was expected this breach would develop into a new pass. For a while it was even given a name, "Charley's Pass," but instead the gap slowly filled with sand, and by 2010, closed completely. Today, the area is deserted and rumored, something I can't personally confirm, to be used as a nude beach. I had read the state's interest in this portion of the island was, at best, lukewarm; apparently, preferring to concentrate on Cayo Costa State Park. I had also recently read in the newspaper the state would like to sell this portion of the island to private interests. I hoped not. I liked it just the way it was. I knew the fishing on the Sound side of this portion of the island was first rate. Fishing was what I planned to do today.

The area is known as Foster's Bay and features one of the prettiest stretches of grass flats in the whole Sound. My plan for the morning was to drift those flats, fishing with either a "Gulp" shrimp suspended under a popping cork or throwing a lure to see if any fish might be interested in that. I began with the popping cork rig, but after quickly putting two eighteen-inch keepers into the live well, I decided that technique was proving to be just too effective. I needed to slow things down. Otherwise I'd have my limit way before lunch and I'd have to find some other way to kill time. So I decided to try casting a top water plug for a while. Honestly, there's probably not a more fun way to fish when they're biting and conditions are right. Having a gator trout explode onto a "Mirror Lure" that you're carefully twitching across the surface is, quite simply, a thrill. I guess it feels like a true contest between you and your prey. Conditions, though, have to be right. The water needs to be free of floating grass and there can't be too much surface chop.

Today conditions were perfect. It wasn't long before I'd boated another couple of trout, one of which was long enough to keep. Again, it was almost too easy, so I decided to try a technique I'd never used on trout before, casting a silver spoon. For this application, I tied a classic Johnson Sprite onto my fluorocarbon leader.

At first I thought I'd made a mistake. No hits. Nothing. The first six casts I used a steady, rapid retrieve, hoping to mimic fleeing bait, but when that didn't produce, I began to vary the speed at which I was reeling in the lure. I'd reel quickly, then I'd pause, then I'd wind slowly. Then, I'd do it all again. This method seemed to produce results. I found as soon as the spoon stopped and began to drop toward the bottom, it seemed to become almost irresistible. Over the next half-hour, I brought seven trout to the boat, but all were too small to keep, which was just as well because I was having so much fun catching them. Finally, I managed to hook a fish I knew wasn't too small.

Trout, once they have been hooked, always come to the surface and roll, and that's what this one did. I'd never seen a trout as large as the one I now had on the end of my line. Its huge yellow-rimmed mouth was gaping open, as the fish fought to throw the hook that restrained it. I knew that thrashing was stretching the hole made by the hook through the tough membrane of the fish's jaw and, if the line wasn't kept tight, the fish would slip the hook through that hole. I kept the line tight. Finally, I was able to bring the exhausted fish to the boat. I slipped a landing net under it and carefully brought it on board. Twenty-six inches long, the largest trout I'd ever caught. With that, I called it a day, and headed toward Barnacle's.

This restaurant is a neat place. It's the nearest you can get on Pine Island Sound to an authentic out-island experience. The primary dining area is under a thatched hut that sits on a low-lying stretch of waterfront sand. Under and around this hut are scattered a dozen picnic tables upon which guests can dine, and/ or enjoy cold beer, much of which is delivered in galvanized metal buckets filled with ice. It's a great place to relax and cool off. And the food's good, too.

I scanned the tables for an out-of-the-way shady table, but noticed quickly I pretty much had my choice of where to sit. So I selected one in the far corner and awaited the arrival of a server. I was hoping that server would be Jamie, a friend of Jill's. She's a divorced mom who works very hard to support herself and her kids. We had gotten to know Jamie when she waited tables at a couple of places on Pine Island, but she had given that up a couple of years ago and had been working out here since. The last time we'd talked with her she'd told us that she liked working here. I assumed she must because she had to get up early to ride the res-taurant's ferry out here every morning and stay late before taking the same boat home in the afternoon. While today the weather for that ride would have been pleasant, I knew that wouldn't always be the case, especially during the winter months. But, I'd never heard her complain. I hoped I'd see her today.

I'd almost given up hope of that when I saw her emerge from the kitchen, a large platter of food carefully balanced on her shoul-der. I waved as soon as I caught her eye. She couldn't wave back, but I knew from the look on her face that she'd seen me. As soon as she unloaded her tray, she came over to my table. I stood up and gave her a warm hug; at least I hoped it was warm. Jill's girl-friends accuse me of hugging them like a cold fish, so I've been trying to work on improving my technique in this regard.

"Jim! It's great to see you. It's been a long time since y'all been out here. Is Jill with you?"

"No. Unfortunately not. She had something to do in town and gave me a fishing pass for the day."

"Good for you. You do any good?"

"Yeah, I did; a great day as a matter of fact. I've already got my limit of trout in the box."

"Fantastic! That's good to hear. Maybe if the fishing gets better things out here will pick up."

"Been slow?"

"Yeah. It has. I know it's just that we're in the slow season now, but still, it's been quiet. Too quiet. But enough of my complaints. Honey, what do you want to drink? You want a bucket of Red Stripes?"

"Oh, hell, no. If I were to drink that much beer I'd have to take a nap and wouldn't get home until after dark. Jill would not be amused. Why don't you just bring me one?"

"You got it. Take a look at the menu and I'll get your order when I come back."

When she returned, I ordered a bowl of black beans and rice and a green salad, trying, as always, not to overeat. When the food was delivered the beans were delicious and spicy. So spicy, in fact, I had to ask Jamie for another Red Stripe. By the time I finished my meal, the only other table of diners had settled their tab and walked down the dock toward their boat. As Jamie returned with the check, I asked if she had a moment to sit down.

She laughed. "Take a look around. It's not like I've got a lot to do."

I laughed, and as she sat down said, "Jamie, I'm interested in what happened to Jay Benjamin. I was wondering if you were you working when they found his body?"

"Yeah, I was. That was a spooky day. We came out on the ferry, and then, about an hour later, one of the construction guys found his body as he was taking a break after he'd put some trash in a dumpster. You can see the dumpster over on that point. Then we could hear that guy start screaming all the way over here. See the ramp that leads up to it? It was kind of funny to see it. That guy started running down that ramp so fast he fell down twice before he made it to the Club's office. We thought he'd seen a snake, or something. Then I guess they called the Sheriff's office from there. Once the deputies got out here and got through talking with him, he came over to get some beer. He was so shaken up I felt sorry for the guy. We ended giving him two buckets of beer just to try to help calm him down. He didn't do any more work that day, I can tell you that! In fact, I've heard he hasn't come back out here at all. Too shook up is what I've heard."

"Yeah. I would be, too. Did Jay Benjamin come out here much?"

"Actually, he did. He and Bill McClelland would usually come out here together. Frequently they lead kayaking expeditions out this way, probably once a month. Sometimes they had adults with them, but more often than not, they'd bring a bunch of high school kids. They'd launch over on Pine Island just off Maria Drive and paddle across the Sound to Foster's Bay. Then they'd wade around on the flats, and Bill would conduct an environmental education class. After that they'd paddle over here, have lunch, and eat ice cream. I have to tell you, I was always envious. I'd like to have done that trip myself."

"Wow! That does sound like fun. I had no idea about any of that. I guess they really were into protecting the environment out here."

"Oh, for sure. In fact, I heard they were working hard to prevent the State from selling the Foster's Bay area to developers. I think they hoped the County would make a park or something out of it. I know they came out here a couple of times with folks from various environmental groups: The Nature Conservancy, The Audubon Society, and a couple of other groups I didn't recognize. But I got the sense from eavesdropping as I delivered food they didn't feel very positive about their chances of preventing the sales from going through."

"Jamie, I had no idea about any of that. Do you have any idea about who's interested in acquiring the land from the State?"

"No. I never overheard them talk about that, but I did hear a couple of the construction guys on the boat ride home talking about that one time. But I don't know if they knew what they were talking about."

"Jamie, what'd you hear?"

"Not much, really. Just a couple of guys shooting the mouths off on their way home from work. I remember one of them said he'd heard a rich Cuban from Palm Beach wanted to buy it. Another fellow said that was bullshit and he'd heard that somebody out of Texas wanted it."

"Any names?"

"Nope. Just what I told you."

"Has Bill McClelland been back out here since Benjamin was killed?"

"No. Not that I've seen. You know I really feel sorry for that guy, after all he's been through."

"You mean losing his friend, Jay?"

"Yeah, that's going to be tough on him. But a couple of years ago, probably about when y'all moved to the island, he was having a really tough time. I know a lot of us were worried about him then. For a while he lost interest in all his environmental work. I guess he lost interest in just about everything. For a while we didn't know if he was going to pull out of it or not. That's why I was so happy to see him and Jay start to do those kayak tours. It was good to see Bill happy again."

"I didn't know about that. Why was he so unhappy?" I asked.

"Well, first he lost his wife- maybe about four years ago. Cancer, I think. They obviously loved each other a lot. I used to see them in town when I worked there. They were one of those couples you always looked forward to seeing again. He'd just about gotten over her death when he lost his daughter. That's what almost killed him. She was a beautiful, brilliant young lady. To show you how smart she was she finished at the top of her class at Stetson's Law School. From what I hear that takes some doing. She'd been out of school only a couple of years, specializing in environmental law, and just starting to get her career established when she died. That just about did Bill in. But something like that would do me in, too. I can't imagine how I'd handle it if something like that ever happened to one of my kids."

"Jamie, how'd she die? Was she ill, too?"

"No. That's partly what made it so tragic. She was just driving home on I-75 one night, apparently fell asleep and her car hit a tree. Killed her instantly."

"Damn! That's terrible. Gives me a whole new sense of respect for Bill, hearing everything he's been through. I hope he's holding up okay after Jay's death. I heard him say they were best friends."

"That's how it always looked to me whenever they'd paddle out here. You want anything else to drink?"

"No. I've got to go. I've got some fish to clean. Jamie, it was good to see you again. Everything okay with your kids?"

"Yeah. They're doing well. Please say hello to Jill and tell her she better be with you the next time you come out here. Otherwise, I might just decide to take you away from her!"

"Ha! I bet she'd say she'd pay you to do that. You be good and give those kids a big hug tonight."

Chapter Twenty-One

Barnacle's sits on the northern edge of a body of water known as Safety Harbor. It's easy to understand the origin of the name since the harbor is almost completely surrounded by land, the only opening being to the east, a direction from which little severe weather comes. Even then the anchorage's eastern side is guarded by a wide stretch of shallow water, water shear enough to strip the power from any waves that manage to blow across the Sound. To enter the harbor deep draft boats have to use the one narrow channel that winds its way along the northern edge of the basin.

Safety Harbor is an interesting place. In ages past it was home to a large Calusa Indian village, and since then, it has sheltered mariners of all persuasions. Spanish explorers, pirates, fishermen, and modern-day boaters have all used this protected basin for sanctuary. One of the things about the Harbor I most enjoy is the old fish shack that sits precariously on pilings at the basin's entrance. It serves as a visible, tangible reminder of the hard living some, in ages past, wrestled from the waters of the Sound. To me, it always seems like there's something magical about this place. I suspect everyone who floats by secretly would like to climb onto its decks and spend a while there, soaking in the atmospheres that seem to surround the place. I know I would like to, but, so far, the house's 'No Trespassing' signs have thwarted that desire.

I had just passed this old house, still deep in reverie, when my eyes focused on a large, fast-moving vessel far out in the Pine Island channel. It was a nice boat, a very nice boat, heading north. I couldn't help but admire it and wonder who could afford to own such a vessel. But then, as I watched it disappear, it dawned on me I might actually know that craft. I couldn't be sure, but it resembled the boat that had almost swamped us a month ago. It looked like the "Sugar!" I put the throttle down and set out in pursuit.

There was no way, of course, I would ever be able to catch it. It was moving faster than I could go in my relatively underpowered bay boat, and it had a head start of several miles. But I could easily keep it in sight; And, I did, at least until it made the turn around Cabbage Key and disappeared from view. That didn't worry me. I knew I'd probably see it again once I made the same turn. I was just hoping it would stop at either Cabbage Key or Useppa. If it headed north to Boca Grande I would have to break off the chase because I didn't have enough time to follow it that far. As I rounded the Cabbage Key curve, I was glad to see a trail of disturbed water leading up the channel to the left, and was even happier when I recognized the large boat tied up at Cabbage Key's longest pier.

As I idled up the channel, I watched the large boat, but I couldn't see anyone on board. I could make out, however, that the name of the boat's stern was indeed "Sugar." I also noticed, moored nearby, a particularly attractive dark green center console. There was a name or diagram, or something, stenciled on its flank, but from that distance I couldn't decipher it. I could see, however, no one was on board that vessel either.

I decided to arrive at the Key as quietly as possible and slid my bay boat onto the small boat beach on the south side of the main docking area. That way there'd be no need to call the dock master and no need to spend time tying up. All I'd have to do would be to ease the bow up onto the sandy shore and power down the stern's shallow water anchor. Normally, I would have also drug an anchor out of the front locker and placed it up the hill, but because I wasn't planning on staying long, I didn't think the boat would likely float away. All I wanted was enough time to have a short talk with the captain of the "Sugar."

As I walked toward the main house, I glanced back at the green center console. Now I could make out the writing on the side of the boat. The symbol looked like it might have been meant to portray a cattle brand, it was a shape I couldn't make out, but the name underneath was unmistakable: "The Royal Ranch!" Well, that was certainly interesting.

Cabbage Key is one of the treasures of Southwest Florida. Originally built in 1926 as a private residence and converted shortly after World War II into a small resort, it has remained almost frozen in time; a reminder of how life in Southwest Florida once was. The only way to reach the Key is by boat. The island features several picture-perfect white clapboard cottages and a main house in which is located a restaurant, bar, and four small guest rooms. It's a nice place to visit, whether you're staying for a few hours or a few days. The only down side being the crowds you'll encounter during the winter and on any weekend. But because this was off-season and mid-week, the Key was not crowded. I climbed the small hill, actually an Indian mound, upon which the house sits, and opened the welcoming wooden screen door. A friendly hostess greeted me as I stepped inside.

"Will you be having lunch today, sir?"

"No, ma'am, I'm not. Just planning to have a couple of drinks at the bar."

"That's fine, Sir. Do you know the way?"

"I've got it covered. Thanks."

I slid past her to the left, stepped up off the porch and into the darkness of the bar area. Even though I was having trouble seeing as my still-shaded eyes had not yet adjusted to the dimness of the windowless space, I noticed a group of men sitting in the back corner of the room. They appeared to be relaxing around a table, preparing to enjoy a round of just-delivered drinks. I didn't look directly at them, but gathered there were five or six of them, and, due to their laughter, it seemed they were having a good time. I walked through the bar and continued on to the restroom that lay off a hallway from the next dining area. I washed my hands, straightened my hair, and returned to the bar with my beat-up, stained baseball cap pulled low over my eyes; eyes shielded by dark Costa sunglasses. It was the best I could do for a disguise. I sat at the bar with my back to the group that was drinking in the rear of the room. I thought it best to listen for a bit before taking any action. And I wanted, possibly needed, a drink or two.

As my eyes continued to adjust, I waited for a bartender to take my order. Once I could see, I slowly turned to try to get a little better look at the men. There were, indeed, six of them sitting around the table. I didn't recognize five of the group, but I did know one, none other than my friend from Red's, the Royal Ranch's Bull. I turned back around to consider that information. As I did, the lady who was tending bar came over.

I expected her to ask for my order, but instead she said, "Jim! Jim Story, what are you doing out here?"

I looked up. I had totally forgotten Anna now worked on Cabbage Key. She used to tend bar at Woody's in St. James City, but hadn't been there for a couple of years. Jill and I liked her a lot.

"Anna! I'd forgotten you were out here. How are you doing?"

"I am great. Couldn't be better. How's Jill? Is she with you?"

"She's fine, but no, I'm by myself today. She had some shopping to do in the Cape, so I decided to go fishing. Then, since I was in the area, I thought I'd just stop by and have a drink."

"Well, you've come to the right place for that. What are you having today? A Salty Dog?"

"Your memory's as good as ever."

"I'll have it to you in a minute." With that she walked away and began rummaging through a cupboard, apparently hoping to find some canned grapefruit juice.

But before I could consider my position further, I felt a hand on my shoulder. I turned to see Bull, extending his hand in welcome.

I shook it, doing my best to act surprised. "Bull, I didn't recognize you. How are you?"

"Doing good, Jim. Truth is, I wouldn't have recognized you either if I hadn't heard Anna call your name. Too bad that good-looking wife of yours isn't here. I'm sure I would have recognized her!"

Having said that, he laughed loudly, obviously proud of his little joke. I didn't particularly like that, but elected to let it pass.

Then he continued: "Jim, come on over to our table. I want to introduce you to some friends of mine. You'll like to meet them. And, besides, I don't want you to be drinking by yourself. That's never good for a man. Come on over and have a seat."

With that he stepped to the next table, dragged a chair over for me to sit on, put his arm around my shoulder, and gently directed me toward the table at which the remainder of the group was now looking in my direction with curiosity.

As he did this, he said loudly, "Boys, this here is my friend Jim. He's the fellow I was telling y'all about, the fellow that accused me of killing Jay Benjamin! Jim, why don't you have a seat with the boys?"

At that point, they all started laughing. I guessed they must have enjoyed the idea of Bull being accused of murder. As I sat down they extended their hands in welcome, just as nice as they could be. Obviously, my plan to act like a bad ass was going to need some reconsideration.

"Jim, it's good to meet you," said the fellow I took to probably be the leader of the group, and possibly the owner of the Sugar. I noticed he spoke with what sounded like a slight Cuban accent. "I don't blame you for suspecting Bull killed that guy. Bull is kind of shifty looking." With that the group started to laugh again.

Then one of the others, speaking with a slow southern drawl, followed up with, "It's not like Bull probably didn't want to kill him. Hell, all of us have wanted to kill that crazy tree-hugging bastard at one time or another."

He probably expected me to join in the laughter that accompanied this comment, but instead, I stood up, looked him in the eye, and said, "Sir, you don't know me, but you should know that I considered Jay Benjamin to be a damn good guy, and I'm sorry he's dead. I want to see his killer put to justice, and I'm doing everything I can to make sure that happens. If you don't feel the same, then we shouldn't be drinking together."

I turned to leave. But stopped when I heard the fellow that I assumed owned the Sugar say, "Jim, please, stay for a moment. I'd like to sincerely apologize for my friend's comment. It's true over the years we have all had our differences with Mr. Benjamin, but I assure you that, despite those differences, I, too, am unhappy he was killed, and I hope his murderer is apprehended. I understand we may have upset you, and because of that, if you do not wish to share a drink with us I will not be offended. But I will be disappointed to not have the opportunity to get to know you, obviously a man of integrity, better."

I looked him in the eye, searching for an indication of insincerity. I didn't find one. Then, after a few moments, with our eyes still locked, he extended his hand, and said, "My name is Raul Faucon."

I realized, after such an apology, that I couldn't insult the guy by not shaking his hand. So I did. And, with that, the tension was broken. Bull pushed me back down in the chair and slapped me on the back. The others, even including the one who had originally made the comment about Benjamin, offered their hands in friendship. I shook them all.

By that time Anna had arrived at the table bearing refills for my new friends and an inviting, icy, salt-rimmed vodka concoction for me. As soon as they were distributed, Raul raised his glass in toast.

"To peace and justice!" he proclaimed.

"To peace and justice!" we all answered.

Damn, I thought to myself, *these sugar barons are sure hard fellows to dislike.*

For the next several minutes we got to know each other. I learned two, including the one who'd said he would have liked to have killed Benjamin, were also sugar growers, both members of the Peninsular Sugar Co-op, and both childhood friends of Raul. One of the others introduced himself as Brian, and said he was from North Ft. Myers. I thought he looked familiar but couldn't quite place him. But there was something about the way his hair was cut, in a style almost like a boy might wear, that made me think I'd seen him somewhere. The style was a blend of influences, somewhere between a butch-cut in front and a short but professional look in the back. And while he exuded charm and seemed polite enough I definitely got the sense he would be happier if I didn't know who he was. The last fellow, sitting to the right of Bull, introduced himself as Mick. I noted that he was a tall, slender, good looking guy with a neatly trimmed goatee, and from the cut of his clothes I decided that he probably had money. And, there was something about the way that Bull deferred to this tall guy, and paid close attention whenever he spoke, that made me wonder if he might have been Bull's boss.

Raul explained they'd come today just to get out on the water, having left from Fort Pierce the night before. With the high price of diesel fuel I couldn't even imagine how expensive a trip like that must be, but I was sure the all-in-cost of their drinks and the cheeseburgers I figured they'd order later would total a lot more than I'd want to pay. Finally, hoping we were now friends, I cautiously suggested I'd like to know more about the relationship between the sugar industry and Jay Benjamin. I was relieved, and a little surprised, that there was no hesitation on Raul's part to enter into that discussion.

"Jim, it is true a long time ago my family, and others in the sugar industry, saw Jay as a true adversary, as someone who had to be defeated in order to prevent him from jeopardizing our industry's ability to successfully and profitably farm our lands, but slowly we began to appreciate his arguments and gradually began to comprehend the damage that was being done to the environment; damage we may have had a part in causing. Most of us, you see, despite how the media portrays us, love the estuaries on both sides of the state as much as anyone. We also could see the harm to our industry's image that was resulting from our continuing to resist reasonable efforts to cleanse the waters flowing from the lake. So for the last two decades or so we have tried to do our part. And, over time, the discussion has shifted away from whether damage to the environment was occurring to who was responsible for causing the damage, and in turn, how much, if anything, those responsible parties should pay to correct that damage. As farmers we think we have more than done our part; we have constructed berms around our fields to minimize run off; we've built green space and retention ponds to control and cleanse that runoff; we've minimized the use of pesticides; and we've recycled our waste products. In that process we have almost totally eliminated our use of fossil fuels. But the public, the media, and our critics give us little credit for our efforts. It seems they still perceive us the only cause for the pollution of Lake Okeechobee. But we believe today that we are responsible for only a minor proportion of the harm being done. If the U.S. Corps of Engineers had not turned the Kissimmee River into a drainage ditch; if the State of Florida had not done everything possible to attract Walt Disney, including allowing it have its own utility district so that it could eventually drain half of Central Florida directly into the Kissimmee ditch; if Orlando and all of its suburbs weren't dumping their sewage waste into the Kissimmee ditch; if ranchers and dairy farmers weren't raising millions of cattle on both sides of the Kissimmee, allowing their waste to flow into that ditch, then the water of Lake Okeechobee would essentially be clean. Our industry's position is that, in comparison, the pollution we put into the Lake is minimal, and therefore, the price that we should pay to restore the Lake should only be a fraction of the total cost. But the media and politicians need a scapegoat, if you will, a whipping boy, and we, I'm afraid, are convenient. To us, the argument is not about whether the environment is being damaged. We understand that it is, and we, too, want it to stop. To us, now, it's just a question of quibbling over price."

"Raul, I see the point you are making, but apparently Jay Benjamin thought there was more to it than that. You're familiar, I'm sure, with his letter in the Ft. Myers' News Press in which he withdrew his support for the Governor's program to purchase Sugar's lands and, in the process, accused the sugar industry of participating in the most massive political corruption scheme in the state's history. Some believe that was why he was killed."

"Jim, what some idealists may see as corruption others recognize as nothing more than the political process playing itself out, just as it always has. I remind you of the old saying that politics and the making of sausage are a lot alike; in the end you may like to eat the final product, but you don't want to watch it being made."

"You are telling me Sugar didn't have Jay Benjamin killed?"

"Jim, I am indeed telling you exactly that."

We looked each other in the eyes again, but just like when I had done that earlier, I couldn't detect the slightest hint of either insincerity or obfuscation. He was either telling what he believed to be the truth or he was one damn fine actor. The eyes and body language of the others sitting around the table conveyed the same message. I know Putin's eyes had betrayed George W. Bush, but right now I was willing to put my faith in what I was seeing. I believed them. It was time to change the subject.

"So did y'all just ride all the way up here for drinks?"

"Not exactly. My friends and I are going from here to Boca Grande, and then tomorrow, we will spend some time in the Pass fishing for Tarpon. I've heard reports that even though it's early in the season, some big fish have already arrived."

This discussion of their planned boating trip gave me the opening I had been waiting for.

"Raul, your boat is beautiful. Once you have seen it you can never forget it."

"Thank you, Jim. It is nice of you to say that. My family is, indeed, very proud of it. My father and my uncle had it constructed by Viking. It is truly one of a kind. The hull is four feet longer than any other boat they have ever constructed. Its interior, engines, controls, electronics, and amenities are like no other. When we finish our drinks, if you like, I'd be delighted to request the captain give you a tour."

"You have a captain on board?"

"Yes. I invited him to join us for drinks, of course, but he prefers to not intrude on our little party. He is a true professional."

I decided to not drag out my mission any longer. The time had come for me to let Raul know what I really thought about almost being drowned by his gorgeous gilded dreadnought.

"Raul, I am sorry to once again be unpleasant, but you need to know that the real reason I came to Cabbage Key today was not to have a drink. The reason I am here is to tell you, or whoever was operating your boat a month ago in the lower Sound, that he is, without question, an imbecile; an idiot. As I said a moment ago, once you've seen your boat you cannot forget it; it makes an impression, so when I saw it today on the Sound, I followed it just so I could tell whoever was at its controls he had almost drowned me and my passengers. If your craft's wakes had not nearly swamped my boat I would have chased the Sugar down and done my best to beat the shit out of whoever was steering it. And I still might. Was it you, Raul, or was it your captain?"

Raul slowly sat his glass on the table, pushing it away as he did. Of course, the rest of those sitting around the table went quiet and sat up straighter. I noticed Bull slide his chair back from the table, obviously preparing, if necessary, to come to the Raul's assistance. But, Raul kept his cool. He slowly raised his hands toward his mouth, his fingers tips together, exhaled, and looked me straight in the eye.

"Jim, you do make it difficult, very difficult, for someone to be your friend. Once again, I find I must apologize. Again, I apologize for the behavior of someone else. I assure you that no one in my family would ever have operated this boat themselves; our insurance coverage and, more importantly, my father's instructions simply do not allow that. So I can say confidently the person you would like to have your discussion with was, in fact, our boat's captain, but I am happy to say, not our current captain. The individual you would like to meet is no longer our employee. A little less than a month ago we severed our relationship with him after we learned he had used the Sugar for a personal voyage, under the guise of testing a repair that had recently been made to the boat. It seems he, his girlfriend, a number of her co-workers at Hendry County's most prestigious gentlemen's club, and several of his drinking buddies brought Sugar up to Pelican Bay for a weekend outing. We only learned about it because an associate of ours, whom we know through my uncle's political fundraising activities, complained to him that he and his girlfriend's clandestine, romantic outing had been most unpleasantly interrupted. He described to my uncle how the Sugar had come into the bay, anchored uncomfortably near his own boat, and then hosted what soon became obvious was a loud, raucous, weekend-long orgy. My uncle's associate was, to say the least, not amused. He assumed, of course, it had been members of our family on board. My uncle, of course, was also not amused. He immediately checked with every member of the family, including me, and quickly was able to determine what had actually happened. He then called back and apologized to his associate and explained what had occurred. Then, as soon as the Sugar returned to its dock, undoubtedly shortly after nearly drowning you and your friends, the captain was relieved of his command and arrested by Palm Beach County Sheriff's deputies. He now faces, I assure you, a lengthy and expensive legal proceeding. But, Jim, that explanation does not really excuse what happened to you and your friends. I can only say, once again, that I am very sorry."

"Raul, I appreciate your explanation, and I accept your apology. None of us were harmed and my boat was not damaged, so I don't want you to worry about this at all. Now that I know what happened, I'm sorry to have distressed you by having brought this up."

"Jim, will you now join me on the boat for a tour?"

"Raul, normally I'd love to see your boat, but this time I need to beg off. I've got a cooler full of fish on board my boat and I need to get them home before they spoil. And I need to get home before my wife gets worried, but the next time we bump into each other, I'd be honored if your captain would give me a tour."

"Certainly, Jim. I understand you need to go. I enjoyed meeting you, and, believe it or not, I enjoyed our conversations. It's not every day I am accused of murder, reckless endangerment on the high seas, and wanton destruction of the environment. It's been entertaining, to say the least. Your drink, by the way, is on my tab. It's the least I can do for what my boat did to yours. I hope you have a good trip down the Sound."

"Raul, thank you. I, too, enjoyed meeting you, and I apologize for all of my accusations. I see now I was mistaken. It was good meeting all of y'all, too."

I walked out of the bar, waving goodbye to Anna, exited the building, and made my way down the hill toward my boat. I was shaking my head, thinking about what had just happened, still not quite sure what to make of it all. Just as I reached the boat, I realized I hadn't determined why Bull was having drinks with Raul and his buddies. I thought about going back inside to insult them one more time, but decided that would have been going too far. Instead, I turned my attention toward how to board my vessel. I'd been inside a little longer than I'd planned, and with the tide coming in, my boat's bow had floated off the beach. Fortunately, the shallow water anchor was still holding the stern in place, but the water's depth at that point was now over four feet. To get on board I had two choices: wade out to the stern of the boat, step up on the engine's skeg plate, and then into the boat; or, wade out to the stern, grab the boat by the gunwale, and swing its bow back toward the beach. With either option I'd get equally wet, so I chose the most direct route and stepped up on the engine; then, thoroughly soaked, proceeded to get underway. I hoped my new friends hadn't been watching

.

Chapter Twenty-Two

"Jim, it's good to see you again. How're you doing?"

"Johnny! Great to see you, too. Man, you are punctual. It's nine o'clock on the dot. You ride your bike or bring the truck?"

"Oh, I just rode my bicycle. Didn't want to burn up gas if I didn't have to. Besides it's only about nine miles down here from Center. That's nothing, especially when I'm sober. Now when I'm heading home from Froggy's after closing time, well, it can be a mite longer ride then."

"I can understand that, but I bet you're sober by the time you get home."

"Yeah. Usually. And I do always sleep good!"

"I bet you do. Now, let's go down to the dock and take a look at it."

Johnny took a few minutes walking from one end of the dock to the other twice. Several times he stopped and bent over the edge, apparently looking at the dock's fascia boards.

"Jim, I got to hand it to you. You didn't screw this up too bad."

"Is that supposed to be a compliment, Johnny?"

He flashed a smile and stroked the length of his beard. I thought I could see the hint of a twinkle in his eyes.

"Jim, no offense, but you don't have a great reputation on the island for your handyman skills."

"What in the heck are you talking about, Johnny? You been talking to Jill?"

"No. But I do hang out at the Low Key Tiki, and from what I've been able to tell, you're pretty much on a first name basis with most of the tradesmen on the island. That tells me something. But the dock's not messed up. It shouldn't take me long to get some stain on it. You've already got the brightener and the stain?"

"Yep. Wood-Rx. Will that be okay?"

"That's good stuff. You know it's made in Ft. Myers and formulated to last down here. Heck of a lot better than that stuff they sell at the big boxes. I'll put it on for you for four hundred dollars, but I won't be able to get to it for a couple of days. Will that be okay?"

"Johnny, we've got a deal. Now, what else did you want to talk with me about?"

Johnny's demeanor changed instantly: gone was the twinkle, gone was the smile. That transformation took me by surprise because, in the years that I'd known Johnny, I had never seen him without them. It was obvious from the look in his eyes he was serious and concerned.

"Jim, everybody at Tiki is always talking about how you solved those murders when the Sheriff couldn't, so I know that you can help me figure out what I ought to do about something I saw the other night."

"When you were riding home from Froggy's?" I asked, attempting to bring a smile back to Johnny's face.

"No, damnit! Jim, this is serious. This is something I saw a while back when I was out mullet fishing."

"OK, Johnny. I'm sorry. I didn't know you mullet fished."

"Yeah. In roe season I do. You can get paid a lot then. The Japanese are crazy about mullet roe. I guess to them it's like caviar or something. Although I never have been able to understand why anyone would want to eat raw fish eggs, but I guess they do because you get paid a lot for the roe. Hell, during roe season everybody usually just takes out the roe and throws the rest of the fish away. Damn waste if you ask me."

"Yeah, Johnny, I'd agree with that, but what's any of that got to do with me?"

"Well, Jim, like I was saying I was out netting some mullet when I saw something."

"You were netting mullet? Were you throwing a cast net for them?"

"No, and that's kind of why I need to talk with you, but first let me tell you what I saw while I was out fishing."

"Okay. Sorry. Go ahead."

"Jim, this was a while ago, but I was in my mullet boat, sitting out in Long Cutoff. I was way back up in the mangroves, just staying out of sight while I was waiting on the tide to turn before I put out my net. Just kind of killing time, you know?"

"Johnny, why were you staying out of sight? And what kind of net were you going to put out?"

"Well, Jim, that's kind of why I need to talk with you. And why I can't go to the Sheriff about what I saw."

"You were fishing with an illegal net, weren't you?"

"Well, how else you going catch enough of them jumping bastards to make a living? I'm too damn old now to spend all night throwing a cast net. And I still have my old gill net from back before they outlawed them. If I'm just fishing for the roe, throwing away the rest of the fish, then nobody will ever be able to tell how they were caught. So, yeah, I was fishing illegally. That's why I can't tell the Sheriff what I saw."

"Johnny, why don't you just not mention that you were using an illegal net?"

"Well, Jim, here's the thing. I've been caught before. In fact, I had to do some time for it. Then I was fishing with a buddy, using his net. They confiscated it. If I tell them I was out fishing at night, they're going to know why I was out there and they won't rest until they take my net, my boat, my truck, and, hell, they'll probably even take my bicycle. So there aint' no way that I'm going to talk with the Sheriff. But, damnit, Jim; I've got to tell somebody what I saw and the boys at the Tiki said I ought to tell you."

"Johnny, I understand what you're saying. What'd you see?"

"Well, like I said, I was sitting out in Long Cutoff, way up in the mangroves, waiting for the tide to turn. You know where I'm talking about?"

"Yeah, I know Long Cutoff. Sounds to me like you were up where it winds around before you get to the power lines."

"Exactly. I was going to stretch my net across the mouth of one of them bayous, and as the tide went out, well then, you'd know, I'd have them. But I was just sitting there, waiting, when I saw what I saw."

"Damnit, Johnny. What did you see?"

"Jim, it's kind of hard to talk about it now. It makes me feel kind of spooky just to think about it."

"Johnny..."

"Okay, okay. As I said, I was hiding back up in the mangroves, not wanting to be seen. It was about ten o'clock, there was a fair amount of moon and the night was quiet. Of course I was paying attention to every noise, every sound 'cause I didn't want to get caught. So when I heard the boat coming up the cutoff, coming up from St. James City, I got spooked. It ain't like there's usually a lot of boat traffic out there at night. I figured it must have been the law and I had to make a decision right then about whether to run or stay hidden, but I decided if it was the law, they'd likely see the wake my boat would make if I tried to run for it, so they'd get curious, follow me, and stop me just for the fun of it. Then they'd find my net and throw me back in the pen. So I decided to just keep hidden and hope they didn't see me, but it weren't the law. You want to guess who I saw, Jim?"

By this time I was getting exasperated with him dragging out his story, but I was also getting curious.

"Johnny, who'd you see?"

"I could see that boat coming a long time before it got to me since they had their running lights on, all nice and legal, and they were also using a spotlight, trying to see where to make the turn toward the power lines. I've got to tell you, that spotlight scared the hell out of me. When I saw that I just knew it was the law. But when I saw they weren't scanning back up in the mangroves with that light, I relaxed and just watched to see who it was out so late. You want to know who it was, Jim?"

"Johnny... "

"It was Bill McClelland and Jay Benjamin. That's who it was. They were in Bill's boat. I could see them plain in the moonlight."

I guess after the suspense from Johnny's dramatic build-up, I was underwhelmed with this revelation.

"So? From what I've heard Bill and Jay were out on the Sound all the time."

"On the night that Jay was killed?" Johnny asked.

Now he had my attention.

"Are you sure it was that night?"

"Yep. I've even gone back and checked the date on the receipt I got for selling my roe at the Fish House the next morning. No question, I saw them together in Bill's boat on the night that Jay was murdered."

"Johnny, you've got to tell the Sheriff about this!"

"Nope. I can't do that. From what I hear, you can, but I'd appreciate it if you wouldn't mention my name."

He turned to walk away, adding as he did, "I'll have your dock done by the end of the week."

Chapter Twenty-Three

I watched Johnny mount his bike and peddle down the street, his beard blowing over his shoulder as he slowly turned the corner toward town. I had to shake my head, thinking I'd just experienced a genuine St. James City moment, but also understanding the importance of the information Johnny had just shared; information that Mike Collins needed to know.

I climbed the stairs to the main level of the house, finding Jill on the phone. From what I could overhear she was chatting with our youngest granddaughter, a three-year-old blond-haired princess with whom Jill shares a special bond. I knew she'd be on the phone for a while, so I picked up my cell, walked back to the dock, and dialed Mike Collins.

"Good God, Story! What is it with all you old farts? Don't you ever sleep? What time is it, anyway?"

"Mike, good morning to you, too. Did I wake you?" I asked, using my most facetious voice. "If I did, I'm so sorry. But come on, man, its nine-friggin'-thirty in the morning; way past time for you public servants to be serving us taxpayers. Or would you prefer I call you back at a more convenient hour, maybe around noon?"

"Cute, Jim. What do you think I do? Keep bankers' hours like you used to? Just to refresh your memory, in case Alzheimer's might have already started to set in, I ain't a damn banker; I'm a detective. And sometimes, and I recognize this may come as a surprise, I do my best detecting after the sun has gone down—long after it has gone down—which is what I was doing until about four hours ago. So this better be good. What you got?"

"Sorry, Mike. But I do have something I think you ought to know. A friend of mine, who doesn't wish to make your acquaintance, told me he was doing some fishing on the night that Jay Benjamin was killed, and he says he saw Benjamin and Bill McClelland in Bill's boat, heading north out of Long Cut about ten o'clock."

"So your buddy was using an illegal net to catch mullet, huh?"

"Why would you say that?"

"Well, it is roe season. I thought all you crackers knew that."

"Sorry. But I can't really say if he was using an illegal net or not. Besides, like an old boss of mine used to periodically remind me when I'd go off on a tangent, that information might be interesting, but it wouldn't be relevant to the matter at hand."

"Yeah. This is good to know and it fits."

"Mike, what do you mean, it fits?"

"Jim, I've got a witness; actually, a fellow you probably know, everybody calls him Walking John. He lives near you in a house down on the bay. Apparently he goes out for a walk religiously, five days a week at 4 a.m., and walks six miles. I guess he likes to get his day off to a good start. Anyway, when he read the Commissioner had been whacked he called to report he'd seen Benjamin drive his car with a kayak on top and park it at Frank's place. He told me Benjamin, after he parked, just sat in the car, like he was waiting to meet someone. John, of course, kept on walking and didn't stick around, so he didn't see anything after that."

"He was sure it was Benjamin driving the car?"

"He said it looked like him, although it was certainly dark at that hour. But he said he thought it was him because the driver was wearing the same floppy sailor's hat Benjamin usually had on."

"So, Benjamin was alive a little after 4 a.m. on that day?"

"Apparently."

"Does that match up with the coroner's time of death estimate?"

"Well, we didn't find the body for a while, so that estimate wasn't much help. All we could tell was Benjamin's head had been bashed in and he'd bled out in the bottom of that dumpster."

"So he was killed there."

"That's the way it looks and that scenario matches Frank's schedule."

"How's that?" I asked.

"Frank's runs always began at six in the morning and he gets to North Cap about seven. On the day in question he hauled construction materials out there and landscaping debris back. He wasn't scheduled to pick up that particular dumpster until later in the week. So I'd guess it seemed like a good place for him to stash a body for a while until he could haul it away later with the rest of the garbage."

"Yeah. That makes sense, but why wouldn't he have covered up the body so it wouldn't have been so easily seen?"

"How do you know that it wasn't?"

"I just heard a guy saw it when he looked in the dumpster, so I guessed it wasn't covered very well."

"Apparently, you have good sources, Jim. But I don't know why he didn't cover it up. Maybe that would have been too obvious. Or maybe he didn't have anything available to throw on top. Or maybe he didn't think anyone would look in there when they dumped garbage on top of him. Probably he wasn't figuring a construction worker would intentionally choose a spot overlooking a dumpster as an attractive place to goof off and smoke a cigarette."

"I can see that. Mike, what about the hat? Was it in the dumpster?"

"Good question, Jim. But, no, it wasn't. It was on the passenger's seat in the car."

"Mike, there's one other thing I thought I'd run by you. I've been told the State is interested in selling the Foster's Bay property on the south end of North Captiva. And my source told me she'd overheard the likely buyers were folks from either Palm Beach or Texas. She also said she believed Benjamin and Bill McClelland were trying to get the land donated from the State so it could be used for a county park or something. I don't know if this might have anything to do with why Benjamin was killed, but to me a Cuban from Palm Beach sounds like it could be one of the Faucons, and someone from Texas sounds to me like the Royal Ranch. Do you think your research assistants could do some networking with their peers at the State to see what they might be able to find out about this?"

"You're just not ready to give up yet on Big Sugar, are you? You're a tenacious bastard, that's for sure. But I'll ask my interns to see what they can find. Jim, thanks for the information. I'll call you as soon as I have anything."

Chapter Twenty-Four

It was Open Mic Night at Woody's. Jill and I had made the decision earlier in the day to attend, but we knew to get a good seat, we'd have to arrive early—six-fifteen or so. Woody's Waterside Rum Bar is the official name of the establishment; a great locally-owned bar and restaurant. Kind of like a tropical Cheers. On any given night there's a good chance you will run into many of your friends and neighbors there. That's especially true on Open Mic Night.

The manager of the place, a great guy named Adam, stumbled upon the concept a few years ago when a well-known local musician needed a new gig after the band he'd played in for a decade decided to call it quits. Rip is the musician's name. He knows everyone on the island. What he really likes to do is write songs, which is a good thing because his voice, after decades of singing, isn't what it once was. So Rip, being ever creative and the unofficial ring leader of many of the area's itinerant musicians, suggested to Adam he could bring in enough talent willing to play only for tips on one night in the middle of the week to entertain the crowd. If enough talent didn't show up, he'd be happy to step up to the mic and entertain the crowd himself. Of course, Rip, for a modest fee, a split of the tips, and free drinks, agreed to ride herd on the circus in order to maintain a modicum of order and decorum. Probably to Adam's surprise, the idea took off. Musicians came out of the wood work. It proved to be, on the one hand, a great forum for new talent in town looking to demonstrate their ability to entertain a crowd, and on the other, a fun place for those musicians who didn't need to play professionally to get their itch for fame scratched. As a result, on any given Open Mic Night there was simply no telling what, and whom, you might encounter, but frequently, the music was amazingly good. We liked to go.

We felt fortunate to secure one of the large round tables toward the rear of the main room. It was a good place from which not only to see the performers, but also to keep an eye on who might be coming and going in the crowd. Within a few minutes, Kenny and Janice walked in and joined us at our table. A few minutes after that our table, as well as all the others in the room, was filled and the first act, a ukulele player of limited ability, started to play. Mercifully, Rip allowed him only to perform two songs before asking the crowd to thank him for his great efforts with a warm send off. He was followed by a banjo and mandolin playing duo, obviously a snow bird couple who had just blown in from Wisconsin. Only two songs for them, too. But the next act was a marked improvement; a cute lady dressed in a fringed leather jacket, strumming a large dreadnought-style acoustic guitar and singing with a voice that managed to bring to mind Patsy Cline.

She was allowed to stick around for four songs, and she got an invitation from Rip to come back and play later. With each act, Rip wandered around the room, gauging the appropriateness of the sound system's settings for each act and paying attention to the crowd's reactions.

By this time, most of the audience had sufficient time to enjoy a couple of adult beverages, and had also placed their meal orders. The waitresses were hustling and the bartenders were busy. It was a happening place.

I'd just finished my delicious barbecue jerk chicken plate when the tip jar was brought by for the first time. I anted up and then decided my bladder could use some relief. I motioned to Jill, who was at that moment engaged in animated conversation with Gigi, where I was heading and stepped toward the rear of the building. I'd just gotten properly positioned in front of one of the two urinals when none other than Bill McClelland walked in and took his spot next to me. I couldn't resist the opportunity to say hello.

"Bill," I said. "It's good to see you again."

"Jim, right?" he asked.

"Yep. We met at Little Lilly's. I'm glad to see you tonight. As a matter of fact, I was just talking about you today with a couple of folks."

"Uh, oh!" he laughed. "I can only imagine what they might have been saying. They didn't call me a crazy tree hugger, did they?"

"No. They liked you, actually. If you got a few moments, when we get through here, why don't we step out by the canal and I'll tell you what they said."

"Sounds like something I should know. See you there."

I stepped outside and walked toward the deck that separates the main building from the canal. During the day this area is usually packed, but when there's music inside, it's deserted. McClelland came out a minute later and joined me leaning against the wooden rail that overlooks the still waters of Monroe Canal. Pelicans and sea gulls welcomed our arrivals with a round of raucous flapping and squawking, a display I guessed was designed to invite us to feed them. As soon as they deduced we had no food, they quieted back down.

"Bill," I said, "I heard today for the first time about what happened to your wife and your daughter. I'd just like to say how sorry I am about your loss. I can't imagine how painful that must have been for you."

As I spoke, I noticed his appearance change. Before I mentioned his loss, he had looked strong and exuded a sense of vitality, but as soon as I mentioned his family, it was almost as if the air had been let out of a balloon. His shoulders sagged, and I could see, even in the darkness, haggard lines begin to appear on his face. Clearly, he was a man still grieving. Then he took a breath, straightened his back, and looked me in the eyes.

"Jim, thank you. I do appreciate your sympathy. It was indeed a difficult period for me, but I have been trying to move on and rebuild. Fortunately, I've had my work on the island to keep me occupied and to give me something else to focus my mind on. Of course, not a day goes by I don't miss them and think of them. I've been trying to do the best I can with what remains of my life, but I can tell you that everything I do, I do for them. Now, what else did you hear about me?"

As he spoke, I couldn't help but feel for the guy and admire him. If I'd been in his shoes I doubt I would have been able to carry on like he had.

"Well, I was out at Barnacle's having lunch and got to talking with Jamie. She told me about the environmental education kayaking classes you and Jay Benjamin conducted. I was impressed. Are you going to continue doing that?"

"Probably not. Jay was really the driving force behind that. Of course, I loved teaching the class, and it always thrilled the heck out of me as the kids began to comprehend the true beauty, complexity, and inter-connections of the ecosystems out there, but I'm too old to lead those kinds of trips. I'm just not strong enough anymore. I wish I was."

"That's too bad. But maybe you'll be able to put something else together. Jamie mentioned y'all were working together on trying to get the State to donate the beach out there to the County so it could be turned into an ecological park. That sounds like a great idea to me. Is that going to happen?"

"Unfortunately, it's not looking likely now. You probably don't know this but Jay and I wanted to do this in my daughter's memory. She would have loved that type of park. Jay was devoting a tremendous amount of his time trying to make it happen. He wanted to name the park in her memory. Initially, we thought we could pull it off. The County seemed to want to do it, but now, it looks as if the State has pulled the plug on the idea. It's the damn Governor, of course. I doubt he's ever set foot inside a park. As far as I can tell, the only thing he likes to get inside of is a set of financial statements. Now, he's bound and determined to have the park system generate enough revenue to at least cover its costs, and, hopefully, generate a profit. The last thing he wants to do is to give valuable land away when it could be sold."

"Can it be sold?" I asked.

"Of course," he answered. "I understand there are several groups who have expressed interest in it."

"Really? What would anyone want it for? I wouldn't think it's really suitable now for building houses or a resort."

"You're right, but, unfortunately, that's not why a group might want it."

As he warmed to this subject I could see he began once again to display the vitality that had been lost earlier when he'd spoken about his wife and daughter.

"Oh, yeah? What would they want to do with it?" I asked.

"Let's assume their long-range plan is to build a boating and golfing development on Pine Island. There are, of course, no beaches on Pine Island, so they wouldn't be able to command top dollar for those properties, but if they were able to also own beachfront property on North Captiva, to which they would be able to ferry guests, pricing would be an entirely different matter. Then they'd be able to ask millions."

"But doesn't the Lee County Land Use Plan prevent them from building anything like that on Pine Island?"

"Today, yes, but The Pine Island Plan can be changed by only a majority vote of the County Commission. There are three commissioners now who reliably vote to block such a change, but if either of them were to be replaced by a commissioner with a different point of view, well, it wouldn't take long before bulldozers and concrete mixers would be heading our way."

"Damn!" I exclaimed.

"My sentiments exactly," said Bill. "Jim, I believe you said in the restroom you had talked with a couple of people about me. So far I've only heard you mention speaking with Jamie."

"You're right, Bill. A friend of mine told me he saw you and Jay Benjamin in your boat, heading out Long Cutoff on the night that Jay was killed. I'm glad I ran into you; I've been wanting to ask you if he was mistaken."

Again, I could see his face and body go through a transformation, but this time, rather than assuming a defeated demeanor, his body became taught, and I saw on his face a look that seemed somehow both cunning and calculating. For an instant, I had the impression I was looking at an angry, cornered beast looking for a way to flee, but that look was replaced so quickly with Bill McClelland's normal smile I wasn't sure I had actually seen what I thought I'd seen.

"Jim, your friend was correct. Jay and I had been concerned for a while about the new shrimp farm that's been built near Center. To hear their management talk, they are operating that enterprise as a marvel of ecological correctness; no runoff, no pollution, in fact, little waste of any kind. To us it sounded all too good to be true, so a number of us had been doing a little espionage just to see if we can catch them in the act of dumping their waste into the Sound. Jay and I, taking advantage of the high tide, took my boat up to where the shrimp farm abuts the Sound. We spent almost all night up there, just sitting quietly behind a little mangrove island, waiting to see what we might see."

"Did they dump anything?" I asked.

"Not a damn thing," Bill replied. "We came back to my house; Bill got in his car and drove off. That was the last time I ever saw him. Jim, you do know he was my best friend, don't you?"

"I'd heard that, Bill. Did you tell this to Mike Collins?"

"He hasn't asked."

When he said that, I looked to see what I could see in his face, but he'd already turned away, staring out at the birds floating quietly on the canal.

"I guess we better go back inside," I said.

"Jim, you go ahead; I'm going to stay out here for a few minutes with these sea gulls. It beats the hell out of listening to that damn ukulele player."

I laughed. "I can't argue with that. See you around."

Back inside I found my chair occupied by none other than our friend, Lillian. I wasn't surprised to see her since she usually accompanies her husband Rucker whenever he comes to play Open Mic Night. They usually arrive late since Rip, for some reason, seems to prefer that Rucker serve as the night's closing act. My guess would be it's because his songs are always both well-performed and funny—a combination sure to leave the audience laughing and wanting to hear more. A great way, if you will, to send the audience home.

I was delighted to see Lillian and, as I walked by, gave her a peck on the cheek. She squealed with delight and gave me gentle slap on the arm—a slap designed to appear as if she were chastising me for my indiscretion, while in reality it was thanking me for the welcomed flirtation. I've always liked Lillian and Rucker. They always seem so happy together. After having heard the talk about how Lillian had slipped off with Frank Osceola, I was anxious to see what the chemistry between them was like tonight. I really wanted to just go ahead and ask her if she was having an affair with Frank, but figured if I did the slap I'd get from her then would be neither friendly, nor gentle. So, I decided, instead, to just observe.

"Lillian, what's the matter? You don't like me kissing you anymore?" I asked.

"Oh, Jim, you silly boy! Of course I love you kissing me," she teased. "Just not in front of your wife."

"Oh, her!" I replied, feigning that I'd forgotten she was watching, before adding: "But she wouldn't mind; she's always looking for an excuse to get rid of me."

"Jim, you'd better hope she's not trying to dump you; you'll never have it this good again, I can assure you of that," she said.

"No question about that," I agreed. "Where's Rucker?"

"Oh, he's around here some place. You know how he gets when he's going to perform. He has to take a lap around the whole place, stopping at every table, getting to know everybody so they'll be looking forward to his songs."

"Yeah, he does that," I said. "Where's Belle? Is she still here?"

I'd inquired about their beautiful, impeccably well-behaved fourteen year-old granddaughter who had charmed everyone in town while she stayed with Lillian and Rucker during her Spring Break.

"No, Jim. She had to go back a couple of weeks ago. We sure do miss her."

"I bet you do!" I said. "She's a lovely child. Did she enjoy her stay?"

"Jim, you just don't know. We did so much stuff together. It was really kind of a magical time for us. We both had so much fun that when she had to get on the plane at the airport we both cried like babies. I can't wait for her to come back," she said.

"I bet," I agreed. "Can I get you a drink?"

"You certainly may. My usual, please."

"That would be a vanilla vodka and soda?"

"Yes, please."

I stepped to the bar and placed the order. When I returned with the drink it was almost time for Rucker to perform. I gave Lillian her drink and stepped to the other side of the table to stand behind Jill. I wanted to have a good spot from which to watch both Rucker and Lillian.

Rucker stepped up to the microphone, receiving a rousing welcome as he did. He talked a little about the type of music he was going to perform; then jumped right into his theme song, a dirty little ditty about a lonely guy's affair with an inflatable plastic doll. The crowd loved it. I glanced at Lillian to see how she was reacting to it. I'd seen her react to it in the past, blushing a little but still beaming with love for her cute husband as he performed. Tonight she was exactly the same. I've never seen two people more obviously in-love with each other than they are. Right then I decided any rumor about her having an affair with Frank Osceola was completely unfounded. From that point on there was no reason for me to ask her if that was true. I had my answer.

Chapter Twenty-Five

The phone rang early the next morning. It was not a number I recognized.

"Hello," I answered.

"Jim, this is Anna. Anna from Cabbage Key. I hope you don't mind me calling you so early in the morning."

"Anna!" I exclaimed happily, while simultaneously giving Jill a shrugged shoulder and raised eyebrow designed to establish my innocence in receiving an early morning phone call from a young, attractive single woman. "What did I do to merit the pleasure of you calling me this morning? Did those guys stiff you on paying for my drink the other day?"

She laughed. "No. They paid. In fact they paid really, really nicely. I've never been tipped that well in my entire bartending career. I hope they come back—soon! In fact, I actually do want them to come back, and, in a way, that's why I'm calling you. Last night the cleaning guy found a briefcase over in the corner near where they had been sitting. All of those guys at the table had been looking at what was inside it, but I guess after they'd finished, it had gotten shoved behind the piano that sits behind that table. I looked through it this morning to see if there was any contact information in it, but the only thing I could find was the name on the outside of the case. It looked like a brand or something and under that was a name stamped in gold: The Royal Ranch. The other day it sounded to me like you knew those guys so I was hoping you might know how to get in touch with them. And, Jim, something else. As I looked through the briefcase I couldn't help but glance at the stuff inside. The one thing that caught my eye was what looked like a set of construction drawings. I couldn't tell much about them but the label at the top of the pages caught my eye. Care to take a guess, Jim, what it said?"

"Maybe something about a resort on Pine Island?" I guessed.

"Damn, Jim. How'd you know that? Are you psychic or something?"

"Not me. Jill's the psychic. At least when it comes to keeping tabs on me. But that is interesting. Everybody's been wondering what they had planned on the island. So you haven't been able to get in touch with them yet to pick up the briefcase?"

"No. I don't know how. I just hope they'll miss the brief case sooner or later and start to retrace their path to find it. Jim, do you know how to contact them?"

"No, Anna, I don't. But maybe if I came out there and had another look through that briefcase I might find something in it that you'd missed. Another set of eyes, if you know what I mean?"

"You want to look at those plans, huh?"

"Anna, Anna, Anna! Why would you ever think something like that? I just want to help you get those plans back to their rightful owner. Nothing wrong with that, is there? I'll get up there as soon as I can."

"Thanks."

"Jill, that was Anna."

"Jim," she sighed, giving me her exasperated look. "I had actually already picked up on that. So, you're going up to Cabbage Key to snoop through somebody else's stuff, huh?"

"No. I'm going up to Cabbage Key to help Anna determine how to return some valuable material to its rightful owner. You want to go with me?"

"Baby, I'd love to, but I think I better stay here and work on some Hooker stuff. The Wine Auction is just around the corner, and we've still got to put together the Silent Auction baskets. Do you think you'll be back in time for lunch?"

"Probably not. But if I get hungry I can stop somewhere on the Sound to get a bite."

"Sounds good. See you this afternoon."

I didn't take the time to load the boat with a cooler or fishing tackle. I was in a hurry to get to the Key before Bull realized he'd left his briefcase there and came to retrieve it. I walked quickly to the dock and hit the switch to lower the boat. I guess it's always a slow process, but today the gears seemed to be turning even more slowly than usual. To make things worse, the tide was out so the lowering process took even longer. If that wasn't bad enough, the bearings that support the whole lift mechanism chose this particular moment to start squealing loudly, probably in protest of not having been recently greased. To me, in my impatient state, it seemed as if they were trying to notify Bull if he hurried, he could get to those plans before me. Damn, I wanted to see those plans.

It took all I could do to obey the 'no wake' rule that restricts speed in the canal, but, I admit I did break the slow speed limit in the bayou, trusting our resident manatees, which the rule is meant to protect, were grazing elsewhere. When I got to the Sound I put the throttle down further than I had ever done. Normally, I cruise at a speed of twenty-five knots (twenty-nine miles per hour); but today I maxed it out at forty knots (forty-six miles per hour). I was in a hurry. Even then it took me almost an hour to reach Cabbage Key. Once there I roughly slammed the boat into a small slip, ignoring as I did the questioning look of the distant dock attendant, threw a simple hitch over the dock's piling to keep the boat in the vicinity, and jogged straight for the main building's door. I ignored the paved path which follows a longer, less steep route up the old Indian mound on which the house sits. Then, just before I threw open the classic wooden screened door, I realized if I stormed into the place like I was about to do, irritatingly saying I needed to go to the bar, my reputation as an alcoholic would be permanently established, so I stopped, took a deep breath, and entered at a more sedate pace.

The hostess who had greeted me the last time I had visited was again on duty. I realized I need not have worried about further damaging my reputation when she asked: "Going to the bar again, sir?"

"Yes, ma'am." I started to explain I needed to talk with Anna for a minute, but concluded she likely wouldn't have believed that story anyway, so I just winked at her and walked on.

"Jim! You made really good time. You must have been flying."

"Pretty much, Anna. Fortunately, there wasn't much traffic out this early. Did I get here in time?"

"I've still got the briefcase, but a fellow who identified himself as Hector called a few minutes ago and asked if his boss had left it here. I told him he had, and he said he'd be by at lunch to pick it up. So if you want to look at its contents you'd better get started."

"Damn right, I want to look at those plans. You want me to look at them here?"

"Don't see why you shouldn't. But it'd look better if you had a drink in your hand. You want a Salty Dog?"

"Why the heck not? Fruit juice in the morning is supposed to be good for you, isn't it? "

"Jim, that's what I've always heard. I'll have it for you in just a minute. Here's the briefcase."

I opened the leather satchel and saw the set of construction plans. I quickly spread them on top of the bar and took a look. The first drawing, labeled 'Buccaneer Bay Yacht and Country Club,' was all I needed to see to understand what was planned to be built on the island. It was a large-scale schematic that diagrammed a sprawling complex of mid-rise condos and luxurious single family dwellings, all situated around an eighteen-hole golf course that wound between Pine Island Sound and Matlacha Pass. I noticed plans for a fly-over bridge spanning Stringfellow Road, apparently designed to allow golfers and residents to avoid any irritating delays as they transited the paved paths among the residences that all lead to a complex of large, Sound-side buildings labeled Yacht and Country Club. In front of those buildings, I noticed plans that showed elaborate dockage stretching into the Sound for three hundred and twenty-five feet. I noted that this wharf featured multiple finger piers, some of which were one hundred feet long. One of them was identified as reserved for the Beach Club Ferry. The drawing indicated that a channel, dredged to a consistent depth of twelve feet, would lead from the dock to the main channel in the Sound, a distance I knew was almost a mile. The whole complex was shown as being surrounded by a ten-foot-high stucco-covered wall. A guarded entranceway provided limited access for residents and guests.

Anna had been attempting, more or less successfully, not to hover over my shoulder the whole time I had been looking at the plans. Finally, she couldn't constrain herself any longer. "Jim, dang you, let me take a look."

I turned them around so she could more easily read the labels.

"Whoa," she said. "Is this what I think it is?" she asked.

"Yep," I answered. "It's the end of life on Pine Island as we know it."

"I was afraid that's what you were going to say," Anna replied. "Now, we better put this stuff away before the guy gets here to pick them up. But, Jim, what are you going to do with this information?"

"At the very least I'm going to tell the investigator who's looking into Jay Benjamin's murder. If Jay had learned about this, it might have been enough reason to have gotten him killed. And maybe I'll share it with Bill McClelland also. It sure seems like somebody ought to know what they've got planned."

"It sure does, Jim, but you be careful, whatever you do. I don't want you to end up getting killed, too."

"I will, Anna. Before I leave let me ask you a question. When I was sitting with those guys there was one of them I didn't get introduced to—the guy with the weird butch cut hair style. But the guy looked so familiar to me, like I should know him from somewhere. Did you recognize him by any chance?"

"Oh, sure, Jim. He comes out here all the time. That was Brian Hutchcraft, the County Commissioner."

"Of course! I knew I recognized him. I can't believe he was out here drinking with those guys and looking at those plans to build something that's not even allowed yet by law. Does that seem right to you, Anna?"

"Jim, you wouldn't believe all the questionable things I've seen go on out here. But, I try not to judge. My job is just to serve drinks."

"I got you, Anna. But, I do appreciate you sharing this with me. Now, I better get out of here."

I made my way down the main channel to where Capitva Pass allowed the Gulf's green waters to mingle with the tannin-stained waters of the Sound before I saw the center console heading north. Even from a distance I could recognize its unusual color and the writing on its flank. It was the Royal Ranch's boat, presumably with Bull at its helm, heading north to retrieve his briefcase. I followed with my eyes the bubbles from the boat's wake back from where it had come—Foster's Bay. That made sense. Since I didn't want Bull to recognize me, I changed course toward the eastern side of the Sound, confident that my change in heading would simply look like I was a fisherman who had just decided to try his luck on the flats near Demere Key. As he passed, Bull showed no sign of having recognized my boat and continued to the north. I stayed on my easterly heading until he was almost out of sight and then swung toward the south, running the deep water that leads to the east of Chino Island. Once I cleared Chino, I steered back to the main channel and followed it toward home. As I drove, I was thinking about what I had just learned, trying to determine how it might relate to Jay Benjamin's death. I was anxious to share this with Mike Collins.

Chapter Twenty-Six

As soon as the boat was safely secured on its lift, I ran inside to find Jill, but I was disappointed when I only found a note she had gone to Janice's house. Apparently, they were preparing for a last-minute cocktail party that had just been called to celebrate the pending unexpected arrival in town of the East Coast Girls, a group of ladies who lived in Broward County and who all had once worked with Janice and her sister, Gigi. From time to time, apparently whenever they felt the need to decompress from the pressures that came with living on Florida's Gold Coast, they notified Gigi they were on the way over and requested she alert the rest of her friends that the party was getting ready to commence. Their visits were always fun.

Before I could even think about joining the festivities, I needed to call Collins. I was glad he answered on the second ring.

"Jim Story, to what do I owe this unexpected and unusually late in the morning pleasure?" he asked.

"Mike… Mike…" I was so excited to tell him what I had learned I was having trouble knowing how to begin. "Mike, damn it, I think I know why Jay Benjamin was killed. I think I know now why the bastards killed him."

"Hey, Jim. Slow down. Take a breath. I've got all day. Now, slowly, why don't you tell me what you've got?"

"Sorry. It's just that I'm so excited. Those Royal Ranch bastards have got to be stopped. I'm convinced now they're the ones who did it. It was probably the big guy named Bull. You need to arrest him, Mike."

"Jim… What do you have?"

I proceeded to tell him about the plans I had seen, and about the meeting I'd been part of, slowly realizing, as I did, I was probably making a fool out of myself.

When I had finished describing the Buccaneer Bay project to the Lieutenant, he said, "Jim, it sounds like a nice place. Are you and Jill going to buy there?"

"Come on, Mike! This could be their motive. This could be why they had to kill Benjamin. If he'd learned about this he'd have raised a stink for sure, especially if he knew they were sharing their plans with a Commissioner."

"So, let me get this straight, you're advising me I need to start arresting everybody in Lee County who has a dream of building a waterfront development just because they've progressed to the point of having someone actually draft a set of preliminary plans for them to show people. Sorry, Jim, but I don't think our jail's big enough for that."

"But, Mike—"

"And, Jim, from what you've told me you had no need, and certainly no authorization, to look at those plans; plans I would guess are proprietary; plans, which, if they were leaked to the wrong person, might cause irreversible financial damage to the development in question; an outcome which, in turn, would likely lead to a lawsuit seeking monetary damages, penalties, and legal expenses, to be filed against whoever had leaked said plans. I sure wouldn't want to find myself, or any of my friends, in that position."

"Well, Mike, I thought you ought to know."

"Know what, Jim?"

Chapter Twenty-Seven

The East Coast Girls welcome party continued far past the normal nine o'clock cut-off time for drinking on the Island. It was almost eleven before celebrations were brought to an abrupt halt by a shouted instruction from an uninvited neighbor across the canal who irritably suggested to those in attendance that it was time to "Shut the F**k up!" As it later turned out, it was probably a good thing he intervened when he did.

Jill and I helped Janice, her sister, Gigi, and Kenny clean up the party's debris for twenty minutes or so before carefully navigating the three completely deserted blocks back to our home. By midnight, we were both soundly asleep; dead, as the expression goes, to the world. And that, as it turned out, was what we almost became.

I've learned over decades of careful research that drinking isn't really conducive to a good night's sleep. Instead, I've found that after a night of serious imbibing, I go usually go comatose for about three hours, but then, after having to get up to take a leak, I have a tough time dropping back off. It always seems that because I've slept so soundly during that first part of the night my body, for some reason, doesn't understand it still desperately needs to rest. And, that's the pattern that played out again tonight.

After my three a.m. visit to the restroom, I found myself tossing and turning. While I badly wanted to drift back off to the distant land of nod, I just couldn't seem to travel that far. Instead, I found myself uncomfortably trapped, for what seemed like at least an hour, somewhere between consciousness and peaceful slumber. Then, after I had finally drifted off, I began to hear the voice, but what the voice was saying didn't make much sense. I thought that I must have been dreaming and rolled over to try to make the sound go away. But it didn't; if anything, it got louder and more insistent. What was it saying? It just wasn't making sense. It had to be a dream.

Then I sat straight up in bed and listened, and this time I heard the voice clearly. It wasn't a dream. Instead, someone outside was yelling, screaming, pleading our names.

"Jim, Jill, get out! Fire! Your house is on fire! Get out! Damn it, wake up. Fire! Fire! Oh, please, wake up, your house is on fire!"

"Jill!" I shouted. "Wake up! The house is on fire. Jill, get up now! The house is on fire."

She sleepily rubbed her eyes and slowly sat up.

"Huh? What'd you say?"

"Jill, put something on and let's go! The house is on fire."

By that time I'd thrown on a pair of shorts and was dragging her out of bed. Fortunately, she'd quickly realized what I was saying, had dressed and had already started down the stairs. I also noticed she'd grabbed her cell phone off the night stand. As she disappeared down the stairs I glanced out the window and could see the reflections of flames. Our bedroom is on the third floor of our home. The main level, on the second floor, is surrounded by a wooden deck. That was what appeared to be burning. That was not good. If that deck was burning, the main stairs out of the house would be blocked. Fortunately, there was also an internal stairway that led down to the ground floor and the garage. I yelled at Jill to head that way and followed as quickly as I could.

As soon as we opened the garage door I saw the man who had been yelling up at us. It was Walking John, the neighbor who habitually makes a six-mile four a.m. trek.

"John!" I shouted. "Thank you for saving us! Now, help us put this out. There's a hose on the west side of the house. You get started with that one and I'll take the one on the other side. Jill, call 9-1-1 and get the Fire Department out here as soon as possible."

Five minutes later we had all the flames extinguished. Fortunately, it appeared the damage was mostly superficial. I thought we'd be able to get back in the house before too long. The fire truck arrived ten minutes later, after having driven down from Center. It was followed almost immediately by an ambulance and a Sheriff's cruiser. The firemen spread their hoses out in a professional manner and began to go about making sure the fire had really been completely extinguished. The paramedics surrounded John, Jill, and me, anxious to administer oxygen, which, fortunately, we were all able to decline.

The Deputy then took his turn. He started by asking me what had happened, but I directed him to John instead, saying, "Walking John saved our lives by waking us up. We'd have died if had not been for him. John, I can't thank you enough for walking by here when you did. What'd you see?"

"Damn, I'm so glad I decided to walk this way this morning. I don't always, you know. It was just luck that I made the decision to come by here. I was just walking along when I heard a bumping sound up on your deck. I guess the guy up there didn't hear me because he just kept doing what he was doing. I looked up and saw a guy dumping some kind of liquid all around your deck. I didn't know if it was you, Jim, committing arson, or somebody else, but I started yelling at him anyway. I'm glad I did because I don't think he got to pour out all his fuel. Instead, he started down your back stairs, and then, using what I took to be a book of burning matches, lit up your deck. It went up in a flash, and I started yelling, trying desperately to wake you guys up. The guy ran toward your dock. I never saw him again."

"Did you hear a boat engine start?" asked the Deputy.

"No. I didn't hear anything, but, of course, by then I was yelling as loudly as I could trying to wake y'all up. I didn't know what else to do. I didn't have a phone to call anybody, and I couldn't get up your stairs. So I just kept on yelling."

"So," asked the Deputy, "how'd that guy get away? Let's go around there and take a look."

Together we walked to the dock, but in the glare of the flashlight's beam there was nothing to be seen other than some grimy looking boot prints that led to the edge of the dock. The Deputy warned us to stay away from them.

"Y'all don't mess with those. We'll want to take pictures of those as evidence."

"Don't worry about that," I agreed. "So how do you think he got away?" I asked. "Did he swim?"

"Not likely with those boots on," the Deputy stated. "Maybe he paddled a canoe."

"Or more likely," I said, "a kayak. You know I sure do keep hearing a lot about kayaks. John, didn't I hear that you told Lieutenant Collins there was a kayak on top of Jay Benjamin's car when you saw it parked over at Frank's place the morning of the day he was killed?"

"Jim, that's not right. What I told him was that there were two kayaks on top of that car."

"You're sure about that?" I asked.

"Absolutely."

"Deputy, I think you better get Mike Collins on the phone. If you have to, wake his ass up! I've got to ask him a question. This is important. Do it."

He looked at me like I'd lost my mind, apparently trying to make up his mind about who he'd rather have to deal with, an angry Collins on the phone, or me, in the flesh. I guess the look on my face finally convinced him to take his luck with Collins. He stepped away and dialed. I could see him talking in a rather animated fashion, and I thought I overheard him explaining I made him make the call. Finally, he walked back over and handed me his phone.

"Mike, this is Jim Story. You hear about somebody trying to burn us out?" I asked.

"Yeah. Y'all okay?"

"We're both fine, but, Mike, I need to ask you a question. This is important."

"Go ahead, Jim. What do you want to know?"

"How many kayaks were on Jay Benjamin's car when y'all found it at Frank's?"

"There was one. Why?"

"Because Walking John just told me he was certain there were two on it when he saw it come by him that morning."

"So? What difference does it make if there was one or two?"

"Mike, that makes all the difference in the world. If there were two, I know who killed Jay Benjamin."

"Who do you think it was?" he asked.

"It was Bill McClelland!"

"Jim, have you lost your mind? You can't just keep accusing people. You've got to have some proof."

"Mike, you've got to trust me on this. Two kayaks explains it all. You know, don't you, that Bill was always kayaking? That's how he was able to get away from my house tonight. And that's how he was able to get away without being seen after he drove Benjamin's car to Frank's. He'd already killed Jay by then, but he dropped Jay's car off to make it look like he'd driven there to meet with Frank. I'd bet that's when he planted the shark club on Frank's barge, too. Then he simply took his kayak off the top of the car and paddled home in the dark."

Mike didn't say anything, but I could almost hear his mental gears spinning as he processed what I'd just told him. I waited. Finally, he spoke. "I'm going to check it out. Put the deputy back on the line."

I handed him the phone. A minute later the Deputy told me that he had been instructed not to let Jill and me out of his sight until Collins told him otherwise.

Walking John then asked if there were any objections to him resuming his walk. The Deputy told him to hit the road. Jill and I walked upstairs to check on the damage done by the fire. A few minutes later we heard the first of what was ultimately to be many siren sounds, all heading south toward St. James City at a high rate of speed.

Chapter Twenty-Eight

Twenty minutes later we could hear the sound of a helicopter coming from the direction of Ft. Myers. As it neared the island we could see the beam of its searchlight, as the chopper slowly worked back and forth in what I presumed was a search pattern of some sort, but I never saw it stop. Instead, it just continued its search pattern out over the Sound, gradually drifting away from St. James City and toward Sanibel. I wasn't surprised that it didn't appear to have found anything. I had to assume that trying to spot a tiny kayak in the pitch-black vastness of the Sound would make hunting for the proverbial needle in a haystack seem like child's play.

By now most of the firemen had departed, convinced there were no smoldering embers that required their attention. Their Chief and the Deputy were huddled together, apparently putting the finishing touches on a required incident report. Eventually, the Chief departed as well, and the Deputy took a seat in his cruiser, carefully positioned where he could keep an eye on our house. Of course, he'd left the cruiser's strobe flashing. He was probably used to the blinding blue intensity of that laser, but we certainly weren't. It was irritating, to say the least. But we didn't complain, understanding in addition to comforting the Deputy, it was serving as a warning to the arsonist who had recently tried to torch our house it would not be a good time to take another shot at us. By now, Jill had made a big pot of coffee, a cup of which I took out to the Deputy.

He said thanks and asked me to tell Jill the coffee tasted good. I was about to turn back to the house when I heard a call for him on the car's radio. He responded. It was Mike Collins; he was on the way over to see us. I waited in the driveway. I was relieved to note as he drove up his siren wasn't blaring and his lights weren't flashing. That would send the neighbors over the edge for sure. As he stopped in the driveway, I walked to his door.

"Jim," he said. "Are y'all okay?"

"Everything is good here. You want to come in for some coffee?"

"Jill make it?"

"Screw you, Collins. You want some coffee or not?"

"Sounds good." He unbuckled, and as he stepped out of the car, took a moment to stretch his back. "Jim, I must be getting too old for this."

"Tell me about it," I agreed.

We climbed the stairs and before going inside, he paused and took a look at the deck.

"What do you think, Jim? How bad do you think the damage is?"

"Hard to know for sure in the dark, but from what I can tell I think it's mostly superficial. Now, come on inside."

"Good morning, Jill."

"It's good to see you again, Mike. Would you like a cup of coffee?"

"Did you make it?" he inquired.

"Collins, give it a rest, will you? But if it'll make you feel any better, yes, she did make it."

"Good. I'll have a cup then." He winked at Jill and gave her a polite peck on the cheek. Then, turning to me, said, "If you don't mind, why don't we sit in the living room. I'm kind of tired."

I directed Mike toward one end of the sofa while I took a seat in my favorite chair positioned nearby. Jill quickly brought his coffee, having remembered he preferred it black, and then stood behind me with her hands resting on my shoulders.

"So, Mike," I began. "What's been going on?"

"You were right, Jim. It was McClelland. You know, this job never ceases to amaze me. A guy like that, a guy who has done so much good in his life, a guy that so many people love—who would ever think that a guy like that would end up killing his best friend, and then trying to kill you to cover it up?"

"So, Mike, what happened? Have you arrested him?"

"We went to his house to talk with him, but he wasn't there. However, he'd left a letter for me in an envelope taped to his front door. In it he explained what he'd done and why. If it hadn't been for you, Jim, I doubt that we'd have ever figured this one out. But let me start from the beginning.

"Jim, you know, of course, that McClelland and Benjamin were friends, and had worked together for years. They were close. And you know about McClelland's daughter being killed in a car accident. That had just about done him in, of course, but he'd finally been able to put that behind him. He and Benjamin were working together hard to get the State to donate Foster's Bay Beach for a park in her honor. Apparently, since she'd died, Bill had never had the strength to go through her stuff. It was all still boxed up in his garage where it'd been placed by friends after she died. Finally, a little over a month ago, he decided that he could handle sorting through those boxes. I'd guess he'd gotten to the point where he wanted to move on, donate what he could, and get rid of the rest. But then he found her diary. Of course, he had to read it. He probably saw it as one last opportunity for him to hear her voice. When he read the last few entries, his whole world changed. He learned that his daughter had been having an affair with Jay Benjamin. He learned that she had been seduced, just like he'd seduced all the others over all those years. And he'd introduced her to cocaine. After all those years of being strong, of excelling in everything she had ever attempted, she'd given in to what he wanted her to do. After reading that in the diary McClelland went searching for the toxicology report from her autopsy, the report no one had ever wanted to share with him before, not wanting to burden him further in his grief, and it showed clearly the presence of a massive amount of cocaine in her system. Now he knew the truth. Jay Benjamin, his best friend, had caused the death of his beloved daughter. From that point on, Benjamin's fate was sealed.

He knew that he was going to kill Benjamin, and when he heard Frank Osceola threaten Benjamin, he realized he would be able to do it without being suspected. He and Benjamin were, of course, looking for evidence that the new shrimp farm was dumping waste into the Sound. So it didn't take much to convince Jay to go with Bill on his boat that night to spy on the place. Then when they didn't see anything, Bill suggested to a receptive Benjamin the idea that the shrimp farm folks might be putting their waste into the dumpster on North Captiva. They boated to Safety Harbor and walked up to the dumpster to look inside. As Benjamin bent over to peer inside, McClelland whacked him on the head with the shark club. Then he retrieved Benjamin's car keys and drove the boat back home. From there he loaded his kayak on top of Benjamin's car and drove it over to Frank's place, feeling lucky to have found on the car's seat Benjamin's favorite hat. He put that on, understanding it might serve as a useful disguise in the event anyone was watching, which of course, Walking John was. But McClelland had seen John as he'd passed him on the road, so he didn't get out of the car until John was gone. Then he put the shark club on Frank's barge, unloaded his kayak, and paddled home. Apparently, he thought he'd gotten away with it until he met you at Woody's. Apparently, the questions that you asked him spooked him. I would guess he thought you knew more than you actually did. Regardless, he decided then that he'd need to kill you, too. But he knew he might not be successful. So, in case things didn't go well, he left the letter on his door to explain what had happened, to clear his conscience, I guess. He said in the letter that if we found it, that we wouldn't have to worry about arresting him. On the other hand, if things had gone as planned, he'd have thrown the letter away, and probably joined in the wake for you and Jill down at Woody's."

With that I could feel Jill's fingers gripping my shoulders a little tighter. I reached up with my left hand, and gave her right hand a gentle squeeze.

"Mike, what do you think he meant you wouldn't have to worry about arresting him?"

"I'd guess he planned to go see his wife and daughter again. We'll start to search as soon as the sun comes up."

"I think I might know where you might want to look first," I volunteered.

"Where's that?"

"Foster's Bay Beach," I said.

"Yeah," Collins replied, shaking his head sadly.

Chapter Twenty-Nine

Several days passed. Jill and I worked putting the house back in order. A few planks needed to be replaced, the pressure washer got a work out, and our backs hurt from bending over to apply a couple of coats of new white acrylic. After all that, we needed a break, and decided a night out at Woody's sounded like just what the doctor ordered.

When we arrived we were surprised by the size of the crowd that had already gathered. Then, once we'd read on the marquee the name of the artist who was playing that evening, we understood why. Pine Island is blessed to have an abundance of talented musicians. And, one of our favorites is a guy who plays under the stage name "Gator." With a name like that you might expect a country act, but you'd be wrong. He is the spitting image, both musically and visually, of a mature Bob Seger. Everybody loves his music. Recently, after he'd joined forces with a very talented saxophone player, that was more the case than ever, hence the size of tonight's crowd. We knew with a crowd like this, it would be a challenge to find a table, but we were hopeful that we'd run into some friends who'd invite us to join them at theirs. That was exactly what happened. As we entered the door, we saw Kenny, Janice, and Gigi waving us toward their table in the back of the main room. We happily joined them.

They, of course, were happy to see us out and about after what we had been through. Apparently, so was much of the rest of the crowd, as we spent the next hour accepting congratulations and drinks from them. Even Adam, the normally reserved manager of Woody's, seemed happy to see us, buying us both a round of free drinks. We were quickly having a great time. The whole time Gator and his saxophonist friend were making great music- they were simply wailing. I would have been happy to have just sat there all night listening to their sounds, but I was too busy shaking hands and accepting offers of free drinks to give them my full attention. Finally the musicians took a break. That created the opportunity for us to talk at our table and actually be able to hear all of what was being said. That was actually a relief. Just as I began to chat with Kenny about his most recent fishing exploits, Lillian and Rucker walked in. We, of course, waved at them to join us.

Lillian happily joined the group, gave the guys warm hugs, and moving on to begin chatting with her lady friends. Rucker did the opposite, hugging the ladies before coming over to chat with the guys. After a few moments discussing the events that had just occurred, he slapped my back and told me how delighted he was we only had a near miss. Then he moved on to other tables, working the crowd in his familiar way.

A few minutes later Lillian came over, bent near my ear, and quietly said, "Jim, I want you to know that I appreciate so much that you believed in me. Jill has told me all about all the rumors of me having an affair with Frank, and how you knew that couldn't be true. That was so sweet of you! And, of course, correct."

"Thank you, Lillian. But it didn't take a genius to figure that out. All anyone had to do was take a look at your face any time you and Rucker were together. But, Lillian, even though I know you and Frank weren't having an affair, I still don't know what y'all were doing that night. Can you tell me now?"

"Jim, I wish I could. But I swore an oath to Frank I could never say a word about what we were doing to anyone. Sorry."

"Okay. I appreciate that you need to honor your word."

I thought then she would walk away and return to the feminine side of the table, but instead, she reached in her purse and pulled out what looked like a photograph.

Then she turned back, handed me the picture, and said, "Jim, I wanted you to see this. It's a picture that Belle sent me yesterday. You remember Belle, don't you? My granddaughter."

"Of course, I do," I replied. "She's got the most genuine smile I think I've ever seen on anyone. Did she have a good time while she was here?"

"That's why I want you to see this. Take a look at the picture and then turn it over and read what's on the back," she instructed.

The photo showed a dimly lit image that I thought, although I didn't know for sure, might have been taken with some kind of infrared device. I had to look at it closely before I could make out the image in the center of the photo.

"Jim," Lillian asked, "Do you know what that is? Can you make it out?"

"It kind of looks like a big cat," I said.

"That, Jim, is the picture of a full grown Florida panther! Now, turn it over and read the back."

I did as instructed and read, "Grammy Lil, thank you so much. This was the best vacation ever. I love staying with you and Grand Pa. And, please thank 'Uncle' Frank for taking us to the reservation to see the Panther. I'll never forget it as long as I live. Love, Belle."

I then looked up at Lillian, but she just winked and left to rejoin the girls.

Made in the USA
San Bernardino, CA
06 May 2017